Moondog over the Mekong

Moondog over the Mekong

stories by
Court Merrigan

SNUBNOSE
PRESS

Moon Over the Mekong by Court Merrigan
Published by Snubnose Press

SnubnosePress.wordpress.com

First Print Edition, 2012

Cover Design: Eric Beetner and Ron Earl Phillips
Interior Design: Coaster Books and Design, Ron Earl Phillips

ISBN-13: 978-0615737669 (Snubnose)
ISBN-10: 0615737668

For Jim Merrigan, 1948-2012.
RIP, Big Bad Dad.

CONTENTS

THE CLOUD FACTORY 11

TWO BROTHERS 17

TWENTY-FIVE GRAND 23

DOGS AT THE DOOR 31

OUR MUTUAL FRIEND 35

A STRAIGHT FACE 49

WE WOULD START HERE 53

CITY OF SCREAMS 71

THE LAST LADDER 81

A GOOD GIRL 89

HARD ENOUGH 101

THE SCABROUS EXPLOITS OF CYRUS &
   GALINA VAN, HELLBENT WEST DURING THE
   THIRD YEAR OF THE HARROWS, 1876 111

MOONDOG OVER THE MEKONG 121

Some of these stories originally appeared elsewhere:

"The Cloud Factory" in *PANK*

"Two Brothers" in *All Due Respect*

"Twenty-Five Grand" in *Pulp Metal*

"Dogs At The Door" in *Powder Burn Flash*

"A Straight Face" in *Spinetingler*

"We Would Start Here" in *Dublin Quarterly*

"City Of Screams" in *Grift*

"The Last Ladder" in *Plots With Guns*, in slightly different form

"A Good Girl" in Porcupine

Part of "Hard Enough (Excerpts From A Bad Life)" appeared in *Off The Record*, in slightly different form

"The Scabrous Exploits Of Cyrus & Galina Van, Hellbent West During The Third Year Of The Harrows, 1876" in *Needle*

"Moondog Over The Mekong" in *Evergreen*

Moondog over the Mekong

THE CLOUD FACTORY

โชคดี

Jimmy brought nothing but a duffel bag. He strapped the bag in the bed of my decrepit Chevy.

"My last ride," he said climbing in the cab. "You're riding home alone, Gary."

"You serious?" I said.

"As a house fire. Take me to the bus depot."

I pulled away from the dirt alley onto the street. We rode past the Dairy King and then out onto the narrow one-lane gravel roads across the state line. Every couple weeks I ran Jimmy in to Cheyenne and downed a couple beers while he unloaded his product. Then we rode back and I came in for two benjamins. Same ride we'd done for four years. Jimmy fired a joint and coughed wet and deep. Yellow skin, clumpy hair. When he handed over the joint you could see his nails all shriveled up. Happens to you when you cook crank. Even though Jimmy wasn't like some crankheads, tweaking in a grubby shanty. He kept his kitchen so clean you could let your dog lick the floor.

I said, "What about your kitchen?"

"Burned it to the ground."

We cruised the gravel, dust snaking out behind us bright in the June sun. On the horizon you could see the big smoke from the power plant just outside Cheyenne eighty miles away. I still called it the cloud factory, like when me and Jimmy were kids. Jimmy tossed a manila envelope on my lap.

"Severance package," he said.

I stuffed it in my front pocket. It was plenty thick.

"For being such a good skate all these years," Jimmy said. "That's twenty grand. Buy yourself a new pickup. Hell, buy two used ones."

"Christ, Jimmy. Twenty grand?"

"Quit your blubbering."

We drove on into the hills, out where there wasn't nothing but cows and prairie goats and cussing underpaid ranch hands. Other Jimmys. He coughed again, his knuckles all cracked yellow.

"So," Jimmy said. "How much do you suppose I have in that duffel?"

"More than twenty grand."

"Bet your ass more than twenty grand. Four hundred fifty seven thousand six hundred and thirty one clams. I counted it three times. Been counting it for four years."

"You loaded a duffel with four hundred grand?"

"Yep. They'll throw in the luggage compartment without even looking at it."

We drove over the old Hamond Creek bridge, tires rumbling on the boards working loose from their bolts. I kept an eye on Jimmy to see if he was sizing up the country at all, saying his goodbyes. But he looked like he couldn't wait to never see them hills again.

"You ain't worried about nothing?" I asked.

He jerked his head. "Why?"

"I don't know. I'm just asking."

Jimmy lit a smoke. He said, "You can smell it on me, can't you." He pulled out a pistol, a sleek little Beretta. "I ought to throw this thing out the window right goddamn now," he said.

"I don't know," I said. "That's some peace of mind you got there."

"Going to get me into a piece of trouble it can't get me out of. You want it?" Jimmy held the Beretta out to me.

"Hell, Jimmy, I don't know my way around one."

"Take it or I'm throwing it out. Here."

I took the piece. Jimmy unlocked his seatbelt and pulled

up his shirt to unbuckle the holster, a neat little job under his armpit. Not even a bulge under his shirt. I looked back to the road. There was a man flagging us down in it.

I hit the brakes and jerked the wheel but the road was narrow and the man went all over the windshield. We skidded into the ravine. The pickup flipped end over end and came up on its wheels. I sat alone in the cab with the pistol cool in my hand. Smoke curlicued from Jimmy's cigarette on the floor mat. Shards of windshield sparkled everywhere. A severed hand teetered on the dashboard.

I unclicked the seat belt and kicked the door open. Staggering outside I tripped into a patch of cactus. I lurched to my feet and stared at the prickers in my hand but couldn't feel them. When I put a shirtsleeve to my forehead, a sticky splotch of blood formed. I unstrapped the duffel bag and slung it over my shoulder. That four hundred grand seemed to weigh four hundred pounds.

"Jimmy," I called.

Jimmy never answered. I found him where he got thrown from the cab and the cab had rolled over him. My stomach jumped and I had to turn away.

I started climbing out of the ravine. My legs were shaky but seemed to be functioning all right. I kept wiping my forehead with a shirtsleeve. It seemed like a real long hike up. On the road a long skid mark sheered into a sizable patch of knocked-down weeds.

Across the road sat a white late-model Lincoln with Texas plates, hazards blinking. The rear driver's side tire was flat and a jack laid on its side by the hubcap. Jimmy would have said the car was one flat away from perfect. Keys jangled in the ignition. A GPS was blinking "No Service" on the dash and the radio was going, some talk show. I flicked it off and unshouldered the duffel onto the passenger seat, shoving the pistol in my pants. I popped the trunk and found a suitcase and in it was a clean white T-shirt and baseball cap.

I cleaned my forehead off as best I could and took off my shirt. The envelope was gone from the pocket. I pulled on the clean T-shirt and the ball cap. Then I got to work on the flat. Little flecks of blood and glass were spattered on my jeans but nothing too noticeable. My hand burned from the cactus prickers.

I had one lug nut to go when a pickup topped the rise. I untucked the shirt to let it hang over the pistol. The pickup rolled to a stop in the middle of the road, brakes squeaking. I lifted a hand.

"Hey, Stan," I said.

Stan looked at the skid marks, the weeds, me. "What the sam hill," he said. "Where's your pickup? Whose car is that?"

"I don't know whose car it is. There was an accident. I don't got a cell signal. Do you?"

"No," said Stan. He got out of the pickup, kicked a toe in the skid marks. "This car was just sitting here? Where's the driver?"

"Down there," I said. "Down there all over."

Stan walked to the edge of the road. He gave a low whistle. "I'll say you had an accident, all right," he said.

I shot Stan in the back of the head. He toppled into the ravine, rolled down into a patch of sage. I went over to his pickup and grabbed a long crescent wrench out of the bed, jamming it between seat and gas pedal. I cranked the steering wheel hard then popped it into drive. About got my arm taken off when the pickup roared into the ravine. I crossed the road and picked up the tire iron and finished putting on the tire. Then I climbed into the Lincoln and aimed for the cloud factory.

A few miles down the road I got to wondering if maybe Jimmy hadn't been bullshitting me about the money. Sixty miles I pondered it. I didn't stop. I wanted all the miles I could get between me and that ravine.

By the time I got to Cheyenne my hands were shaking good. I kept them in my pockets walking into the truck stop. Felt like every son of a bitch in the place was eyeing me. I requisitioned a private shower room and set the duffel bag down beneath a mural of penises scratched into the wall. I opened the duffel up. Jimmy was a good skate. The money was there, all right. Stacks of bills beneath books, T-shirts, tube socks and a Greyhound ticket. Also a billfold with a California state ID and no picture. David Shandy.

"David Shandy," I said to myself. "Dave. Nice to meet you."

The mirror in the place had been removed so I cleaned up best as I could by my distorted reflection in the paper towel dispenser. I buried my old billfold deep in a trashcan filled with mushy paper towels and palmed a few bills from a stack, slid them in my new billfold and stuffed the Beretta in a tube sock. At the front I bought a Coke and some beef jerky and drove downtown to the bus depot.

I parked the Lincoln at a Piggly Wiggly, threw the keys in the trash and walked to the bus depot. At the booth I slid the ticket through the slot to the lady. I could just make out my face in the scratched security glass. I tried to see if I was the same or not. It was hard to tell. Then I noticed the lady behind the glass talking to me.

"Sir? Las Cruces, sir?"

"What?" I said.

"Las Cruces. Your destination, sir. Is that correct?"

"Yeah," I said. "Las Cruces. That's right. That's where I'm headed."

"Have a seat in the waiting area, sir," said the lady.

I had a seat in the waiting area, feet on the duffel bag. Some news show was on making no sense so instead I watched the cars go by on the boulevard, watching for dents and cracked windshields. When it came time to get on the bus, I let them stow the duffel in the luggage compartment below, like Jimmy said. He was right. No one even looked at it.

TWO BROTHERS

สิ้นหวัง

Narin's bird took a mauling at the cockfights that would require many weeks of close tending to heal. Narin didn't mind. He'd made out well, bills bunched in his front shirt pocket. This bird was a good ringer, putting up a vicious feint and attack show that was nothing but prelude to inevitable defeat, useful for goading new cockers into overconfidence on their birds. Riding back to the freehold on the motorbike, Narin handled the cock with a tenderness due a newborn baby. The nubs of his fingers throbbed but tonight it didn't bother him. He had plenty to tell his little brother Taem.

Now that his daughter Phrae was gone, Taem liked nothing more than to hear about the cockfights. He would nod along, eyelids blinking over empty sockets, jabbing the air with jerky fingers, sucking his teeth and throwing up his arms in a paroxysm of defeat or victory. Phrae used to giggle watching. But she'd left on a bus for Bangkok two months ago, Narin narrating the departure for Taem as the midday sun curled the tar in the joints of the highway.

Taem spent his days perched by a cracked transistor radio, listening to old songs through AM static, rolling palm leaf cigarettes, stroking the birds that wandered the cock house. A dozen times a day, he disassembled a tarnished .38 revolver, laying the pieces out in sequence, oiling the apertures and surfaces. Every so often he would unleash a series of gravelly grunts, keeping it up until Narin took the .38 and fired it. The cocks were used to the racket, didn't even squawk. Taem would quiet and take back the warm piece to stroke and reload.

Narin started substituting blank reloads because he worried Taem would accidentally shoot off his foot or worse. He made two vows in his daily obeisance to the household Buddha: to see to little Phrae's future, and to never see his brother's blood again, not in this or the next ten lives.

—§—

When their father and mother died in a motorbike accident, Narin took over the family barber shop in Prachinburi, two hundred kilometers from Bangkok. Taem, meanwhile, bolted for Bangkok the day after the cremation.

Narin worked the barber shop for nineteen years. Weary of the stinking mound of hair he burned each evening, in 1983 he sold up and moved to Bangkok. There he went into business building steel window frames for shophouses and tract homes. Narin was deft with his hands, long fingers graceful about a welding torch, so the money was steady. He sent for his wife after he fixed up the rooms above the shop. But she was a country girl and balked at Bangkok's smoke and noise and the indecent sitting toilet, so unlike the proper squatter back home. She quickly returned to Prachinburi but the separation was amicable. Narin sent money for a while, then stopped, and they did not see each other again.

A few months later, Taem sauntered into his shop.

"Well, big brother," said Taem, looking at the neatly stacked rows of freshly-painted steel frames. "You're doing well for yourself."

They talked a while about the old days, but soon Taem was going on about his woman, his apartment, his job. He was a deliveryman and he was making out good. One day he'd see his way clear to a detached house and a black car and gold necklaces for his woman.

"What's her name?" asked Narin.

"Samnien," Taem said. "You'll like her. I'll bring her around sometime."

Narin never did meet Samnien, never got one look at Phrae's mother. Later he would try to see her in Phrae's face. He couldn't.

Taem was soon a fixture at the shop, perched atop a steel desk watching Narin work, warbling along to old songs on the radio. He talked to customers. He was good with them. He'd laugh and joke and offer cigarettes and fetch cups of water and if there was a kid, Taem would pull coins and string from their ears and they'd shriek with laughter.

Every hour he made a call on the shop phone and once or twice a day, he'd strap on his green backpack and zip off on his motorbike.

"Not bad work, huh," he said to Narin, and Narin agreed. "Tell you what, you should have seen the last place I had to hang out in. Real shithole. I got it good here, brother."

—§—

Taem was a drug runner, employed by one of the syndicates that had Bangkok divvied up. Pay came in rubber-banded bundles of cash, more than enough to keep Samnien in the two-level apartment but not enough to get her a car. He had to pay off the cops, too, who made a great show of putting him against the wall and patting him down, even though they knew exactly how much they were coming in for. The rates were set by the syndicates. The only annoyance was the occasional necessity to pistol-whip a deadbeat with the .38, kick him to the cops for their monthly arrest quota.

Taem never fired the .38 until that day in mid-1985 when a couple of syndicate members thought he was getting uppity and snatched away his money bundle, and in the close cement room down a back alley three blocks from the Turkish embassy Taem shot both of them dead. Back at Narin's shop Taem made call after call but no one answered. He sat on the desk chain-smoking and ignoring the radio, nearly backhanding some kid who wanted a magic show.

—§—

They came for Taem in the middle of the night. Kicked him in the balls and drug him out of the two-level apartment in boxers, Samnien screaming. They didn't say anything. They knew who he was. They knew just what he'd done.

—§—

When Narin sprinted downstairs into the shop, summoned by Taem's screams, he was invited by the three men standing there to have a seat. He did, and was lashed to a welding table, arms out.

Taem couldn't keep to his feet. The men let him flop to the floor, naked, every orifice bleeding, including the emptied eye sockets. They had used chopsticks and a spoon for that.

One of the men took a snipping tool from Narin's workbench and sheared off both index fingers at the first knuckle. Then the man used a blowtorch to suture the spurting wound. He was skillful with both. He had done this before.

"Now," the man said. "Let's see if you know any more than your brother here."

Narin did not, though he was not believed until the snipping and suturing was repeated on each of his fingers and both big toes.

"Well, boys," said the man. "What the fuck, huh." He steadied Narin's lolling head, whispered in his ear like a lover. "If I were you, I'd get the fuck out of Bangkok."

—§—

Narin convalesced two months at the Sisters of Mercy hospital in Prachinburi, listening to Taem moan, watching him flail and punch air as he tried to ward off invisible attackers in his dark ether. When the nuns finally released the brothers, Narin took the cash he'd plucked from the shop safe and bought the little freehold on a scrap of waste ground deep in the countryside. There he learned with excruciating slowness to utilize his finger nubs, pouring concrete, building the hut and the cock house out of bamboo and palm leaves. He bought Taem the radio and left his little brother listening in the shade of the palm trees.

One day a postcard frayed at the edges found its way to the brothers. It was from Samnien. It had been some months in transit and it said Taem had a daughter.

Narin located the charity hospital in Thonburi, across the river from Bangkok. He found the baby squalling in dirty cloth diapers in a bassinet she shared with two other infants in a vast orphanage hall where hundreds of such infants mewled. The overhead fans had ceased working years before and the swarms of flies were audible from the stairwell. The infant's skeletal body was stippled in sores, her eyes yellow as a Buddha idol. Narin knew the child was Taem's when he saw how she flailed spasmodically every minute or so, as if imitating her father.

The girl was five months old, possibly six, or nine, or eleven. No one knew for sure. The records had been misplaced. Samnien had abandoned the child the day after it was born. One nurse remembered Samnien saying she feared for her life and that the child was cursed.

Narin filled out the forms, named her Phrae, and brought her home.

Both infant and father calmed when Narin handed her over. Narin left them together thereafter, the blind man rocking and singing, the silent infant staring at him. Taem fed her out of his own bowl, mashing fish and rice in his fingers, and slept with her curled into him on a bamboo platform. When nightmares bolted Narin awake in the deep night, he listened to their placid breath until he could sleep again. Between occasional cockfight winnings and day labor, plus the little garden Phrae planted and weeded, they stayed in rice and kept Phrae in school uniforms and books and oil for her study lamp. The whip smart little girl was fast becoming all the brothers could have hoped. She won the top government scholarship of 2003 and now she was in a lonely dorm bed in Bangkok, bright future unfurling before her.

—§—

Narin pulled up at the little bamboo and thatch hut on the freehold. He killed the motorbike and squatted on the slab of rough concrete by the spigot in front of the cock house. He switched on a naked light bulb and rubbed down the cock's head with an old rag, staunching the bleeding about its horny scars, squeezing open its beak with thumb and forefinger and running a feather down its throat to extract blood and mucous. He hummed an old song. The cock was mute.

Squawking came from inside the cock house. It sounded like a couple of cocks were out. Strange—Taem was religious about putting them away in the evening. Narin pushed open the bamboo gate.

"Taem?" said Narin, squinting into the darkness. "Taem?" He found the light switch and squinted into the glare. "Oh, shit, Taem," he said, and kicked aside the two escaped cocks.

Taem lay on his side, putting the .38 against his temple and dry-firing, over and over. He had emptied the chambers earlier that evening, barrel hot to his head. The reverberation of the blank reloads perforated his eardrum. Blood seeped from his ears and the two escaped cocks attacked the red rivulets.

Narin gently righted his little brother. Why, he wondered, then stopped. How useless such questions, all questions. He put his brother's head to his chest and murmured one of the old songs.

TWENTY-FIVE GRAND

ขี้ขลาด

Wanissa doesn't have an address cabbies will go to. Three of them shake their heads and drive off. The fourth thinks a long while before letting us in. We cross the river and the cabbie tells us he doesn't often get a fare to this part of the city. People who go there, he says, take chauffeured Benzes. The ones that live there take the bus. This doesn't strike me as an especially good sign.

Wanissa was introduced to me as a friend of my wife's family. My wife's family has plenty of fingers in plenty of rice bowls. That's why I agreed to lend Wanissa the money. She said she needed it to buy new sewing machines. To keep her garment business afloat. So I could be forgiven for thinking I made a business loan. Seemed secure enough. Up until yesterday, that is. When I found out that by "friend of the family," my wife meant "former maid."

I wouldn't have lent the money to Wanissa if I'd know she was or ever had been a maid. No, you can't trust the poor. Especially here. A sad fact, but a fact all the same. Poor people with ambition, they find a way and don't stay poor. The rest of the unfortunate bastards, they just don't understand and you can't make them. If you want to piss your cash away, let them touch it.

I have also discovered that by "come to Bangkok to see me as often as humanly possible," my wife means "come only when I specifically ask." She's not very happy about my sudden appearance. I called her just before I caught my flight. She's my wife. How much warning do I have to give her? But she acts like meeting me at the airport and spending the night together (our first in two months) is a long boring workday and she's counting minutes till the five-o'clock whistle.

We've lived apart since we got married. My wife isn't exactly rushing me to join her, I'm noticing. I've been planning to move here to Bangkok for a while now, but my declining fortunes are keeping me busy in Japan. Turns out, I can use those monthly installments on the loan. That's why I'm here. Wanissa made exactly one payment. And nothing in the six months since then. So I'm going to see her. Have a chat. I've brought along Suthon. Suthon I trust. I knew him before I met my wife. I don't have much practice at this loan-collection thing. Suthon does.

Now, not all that long ago, twenty-five grand in American dollars wouldn't have been that big a deal to me. But my affairs keep heading south. You'd think the sex trade would be recession-proof. In hard times a man tightens his belt, lowers his eyes, and goes home to fuck his wife. Which creates problems for me: I recruit girls for the Japanese market. From hostesses to strippers to fetish girls to hookers, black and white and yellow and brown, I bring them in.

Willing girls only, mind you. I find as of late I have to clarify this point. I'm no slave trader. Hell, this business is how I met my wife. Her family owns a string of "massage" parlors. Hence their maids. Hence Wanissa. Hence me taking time off to come down here and chase down my money. And, as a sideline project, to see my wife. Slip back inside matrimonial bounds myself for a few days.

We creep our way through the choking traffic, and eventually get off the main streets. Christ on a crutch. Look at this. Like a war zone. Crumbly gray concrete tenements, half-covered in hanging rags. Laundry, I suppose, although nothing I'd put on my back; most of it looks unworthy of a toilet rag. I doubt any of these buildings have ever encountered a paint can They're colored in creeping black decay and rusty streaks, with networks of spidery cracks for trimming. The streets are so narrow pedestrians have to step aside and bicyclists have to dismount so we can pass. The tires crunch over plastic and paper and rags and bricks in the refuse-packed streets. Sinkholes all over the road, jagged chunks of asphalt collapsing into them.

Young girls wander the streets. I watch them. Who knows? Someday I could be their conduit to a better life. Happens all time. Sort of rewarding, really. Besides, only the gutter snipes ever really appreciate what you do for them.

Half-naked kids sprint in front of the taxi. One little tyke's attire consists of purple rain boots, useful for tromping through streams of fetid run-off and open sewers. The taxi driver slams on the brakes and misses his bald head by about a bumper. He's lucky, after a fashion. The little survivor and the rest of his gang of semi-clad buddies gape as we go by. The side of his face is covered in purple boils.

The cabbie keeps going. It becomes increasingly clear he has only a hazy familiarity with the area. I just manage to stay quiet. The cabbie deserves a mouthful but there's no point. Eventually, smiling while not apologizing, he stops in front of a dilapidated store. Which stocks, from the looks of it, used motor oil and beer. A bulbously fat Chinese-looking man, mole on his jaw sprouting a six-inch long gray hair, babbles some directions at him.

A few more twists and turns, enough to wreck my last notions of orientation, and we find the place. It's not really a place. It's a mud lot, where a building got torn down about a decade ago, now jam-packed with squatter hovels. One of them must be Wanissa's.

So—I lent this woman twenty-five grand. To be paid back in generous installments, at a very fair rate of interest. And this is where she lives? Where's the garment business, do you suppose? Those sewing machines? She's running a sweatshop out of a tin hut, is she? I can call this a lot of things. I'll call it the last time I take my wife's word. My own damn fault. I should married a plain honest girl from, I don't know, Cleveland. Tuscaloosa. Salt Lake City.

Suthon and I get out. I tell the cabbie to wait. Not likely another cab will be coming by any time soon. A crowd of filthy waifs gather around us. One of them has a soccer ball. He kicks it and the ball hits me in the shin, leaving a black imprint on my cream trousers. I don't even want to think about where that ball's been. Suthon scatters the kids with a few phrases and looks. They keep the staring up from a distance. I guess we're a sight to be seen in these parts. Me: balding white dome awash in sweat, bulging belly hiding my toes, backs of my hands already going speckled, two-day beard disguising an ever-growing network of wrinkles. Suthon: stocky and dark, muscles rippling in the right places, slicked-back hair, tailored clothes.

Which hovel is Wanissa's, then? Must be a hundred of them. I'm not going to pop into each one asking direction. Suthon gets on it.

Efficiently, he heads straight to the moms. A pair of them, to be exact. Fat, soon-to-be toothless, prematurely middle-aging. Wrapped in sarongs, flesh peeking over every fold, each with a listless baby that looks too old to be held but probably isn't strong enough to stand. They tell Suthon six hovels back, on the left, past the tilted-over lamp post, next to the upright concrete slab with the obscene graffiti.

Easy enough. There it is. Maybe six foot by ten. Walls of tin siding, plywood roof. A rusting Iowa license plate and a Manchester United banner, edges frayed and streaked with faded red, hang over the entrance. A thin blue tarp hangs over it, stolen from a market or construction site. I rap on a wall. There's shuffling around inside. I push the tarp aside and go in, ducking under the splitting two-by-four holding up the entranceway. Now's no time to stand on formality.

After the slanting glare of the pollution-refracted sun outside, it's pretty murky in here. A sickly lamp in the corner, sparking and dimming. With the notches of light coming in from the corners, there's just enough light to mostly see.

A man is halfway standing up from a fruit crate. He's staggered by our arrival. So much so that juice is running off his knuckles from the ripe mango he's squeezing. He has two boys by him. Both under ten, probably, although so covered in filth it's hard to tell. One has on a piss-yellow Winnie the Pooh T-shirt and checkered shorts. One has just the shorts, identical to his brother's. The man has no shirt and his skin hangs in flabby folds off his arms and droops in greasy torpor over his belt. His cracked yellow fingernails are long enough to be spoons. Oily hair lanks around his dark face. His lips are flaccid meat curtains.

He looks petrified. I'll bet he is. Right away he starts blathering. My Thai's not bad, but it's not up to deciphering his gibberish. I tell him to calm and sit down. I mention who I am, and who my wife's father is. This makes an impression. I say that I'm a business associate of his wife Wanissa. I explain his wife and I have certain financial understandings, which may or may not concern him. Which isn't my concern. I want to know two simple things: where is Wanissa, and where the fuck is my money. Suthon takes up a strategic position by my side.

The man sits back down on his crate. He calls the boys to his side. They kneel beside him and he puts his arms around them.

"I haven't seen her in months," he says. "Please. Believe me."

"Are these your children?" I ask. "Yours and Wanissa's?"

"Yes. Please, sir. Please."

"Do you have any idea where your wife might be?"

"No," he says. "She left us. She took everything. Even the electrical cords. I lost my apartment. My motorbike. Wanissa hadn't paid anything in months. And then a drunk trucker wrecked the factory van I used to drive. I got fired. I owe the company damages. We came here. We have nowhere else to go. I'm the one who gave this address to your wife."

I let him go through it. Hard to say whether to believe him or not. Though it hardly matters.

"My money," I ask. "How about the money?"

"I don't know anything about your money," he says.

He puts his head in his hands and sobs. Well, there are any number of ways to usefully jog a memory. Suthon is stepping to it. Then, from behind the greasy curtain dividing the shack in two, steps a girl. Out of professional interest, I hold Suthon back.

My assessment takes about two seconds. This girl got pock-marked cheeks, crooked overbite, nose splayed like an over-the-hill heavyweight's——I'm sorry her face happened to her. Although she does have fantastic eyes. Black as fired obsidian, whites like glacial snow. Steady as a crystal. Something primeval in them.

Piled on her face is a grimy layer of horrifically misapplied makeup. Which comes nowhere close to making her look any older. She could be thirteen or possibly fourteen. She's wearing a uniform, gray, factory-issue. Stained with the chemical byproducts of a multinational corporation which likely has achieved product placement in your household. The trademark is on her breast pocket. I know all about it. A girl I got a gig in Japan used to work in one of those factories. For seventy hours a week, she was paid almost a living wage and managed to escape with no significant bodily injury and enough intact beauty to be a popular draw in a hostess club. Where, I might add, she makes twenty times as much.

Like the poor everywhere, at whom life has already tossed so much misery and bullshit that nothing's shocking, the girl seems unsurprised by the scene. She goes over to her father. She put her arms around his shoulder. He takes his hands away from his head and wraps them around her waist. The sons snuggle in closer. They are crying, too.

She's not. She looks down on these sorry males, for all the world like they're her brood. She whispers something to them. Then she looks at me. Her eyes are smoldering finely. A few million years of evolution are plainly on her side. If anyone in this shack knows anything about my twenty-five grand, no one going to say now.

I repeat myself. For form's sake. The girl shakes her head. Her father won't look up. I can see Suthon would like to engage in more vigorous questioning. But no. You can't put the squeeze on people who've got nothing, can you?

I promise to be back. Suthon and I back away. I trip on an empty bottle on the way. Nearly fall over. I have to clutch at a wobbly shelf to keep my balance. There goes the last of the fear and awe. The girl keeps staring. Her sorry men keep crying.

Winding our way back through the hovels, Suthon says he'll stay on it. I can see he's not happy about this. Nope, I can't seem to please anyone. The taxi's there.

"How about that?" I say to Suthon, back in the air conditioning.

He shrugs. "Possibly they know nothing," he says. "But you are too kind."

"Too chickenshit, you mean."

Suthon doesn't answer that. "I'll go back," he says. "When you will not have to watch."

Wish I could do something for the girl. Considering what Suthon's going to do to her family. I think of asking him to refrain. He will if I ask. But I don't. Like I said, times are tough. I need that twenty-five grand.

DOGS AT THE DOOR

จำเป็น

The dogs hurl themselves against the camper door with maniacal intensity. The tips of their snouts snick through the gap with pink flicks of tongue, paws clicking as they bark in short rasps. Their black coats are spangled with raw pink sores. They are starving.

Six year-old Axel sits on his knees in the camper strewn with newspapers and empty beer cans and candy bar wrappers. One of his mother's tennis shoes leans half upright in a corner, untied. His mother is slumped next to him. She has been dead all day.

That morning he sat hunched on a rock outside by the fire ring, watching Mama set bacon on the camp stove.

"Have to get myself handled," she said. "Cook that bacon up."

She went in the camper with a baggy. Axel tried to get the camp stove started but it was out of fuel. He did not call out. He hunkered down to wait, as he'd done with C.C. in the backseat of cars, in strange garages, in public parks on rusting swings. Waiting until Mama and Dad came staggering back to head out for wherever was next. Dad would pick C.C. up and sing walking back to whatever car they had this time.

Yesterday it was a rest stop. Folks clutched tight to their kids' hands going by where Axel and C.C. sat at a cement picnic table playing tic-tac-toe with flecks of limestone. When Mama and Dad came out of the trees they were screaming. Mama pulled out clumps of her own hair and battered Dad in the face with the hair clutched in her fists. Dad walloped her good and she went sprawling.

"The hell with you, woman," Dad said.

Dad picked C.C. up and threw him in the backseat, bonking his head on a window. Axel watched C.C. crying in the car window as Dad burned rubber for the interstate. Mama stayed stretched out on the grass, crying in shuddering catches. Axel waited. People kept on passing wide. Finally Mama sat up.

"You're the onliest thing I've got," she said.

She limped to the phone booth and that was how they ended up here, in the woods just off some crossroads. Next to a scrap yard where those starving black Dobermans burrowed under the fence.

When the dogs tire of throwing themselves at the door, they rest, heads on paws. Axel watches through a cracked plastic window. He does not blame them. His stomach yowls. He knows how they feel.

At sunset they are still there. Every so often they snuffle up to the door. He falls asleep leaned against Mama. Mama gets colder as the night wears on.

In the morning the dogs are still there and Axel licks the dew on the walls. He pisses carefully into a styrofoam cup. Dad always said there might come a time when you have to drink your own piss.

Axel waits all day, listening to the traffic at the crossroads. At nightfall the dogs began pawing at the door again. He adds a dribble to the cup then drinks it off. It tastes better than the walls. For a few minutes the edge of thirst is blunted. Which only put his guts through the wringer. He sits cross legged next to Mama and tries to cry so he can lick the tears but no tears come.

—§—

The dogs sleep, black lumps in ragged moonlight. Axel slides the door open and stands looking. Mama's tennis shoe is heavy in one hand. He steps down, sneakers silent on the damp pine needles. He hurls the shoe back inside the camper. The corrugated aluminum rattles. The dogs' heads shoot up as if on wires. They scrabble for the open doorway, snarling for the corpse.

Axel runs as fast as his pumping little legs will go, the doorway behind like a portal from one of his Flash Gordon comics, headed for the highway, the lights of the crossroads. Not so fast that he does not hear fangs ripping into cold flesh, that will someday be almost all he can remember of Mama.

OUR MUTUAL FRIEND

ครอบครัว

NATTY ELSINORE

I pull around back of Power's Tire Shop to employee parking, get out, look in the car. The air reeks of boiling blood from the slaughterhouse across the highway. A kid-sized fishing pole still in the wrapping is laid in the back seat. I'm a little surprised he's not more circumspect. Maybe suddenly having a family makes you careless. I wouldn't know.

I drive back around front and carefully hike up my skirt, undo the top two buttons on my blouse. I walk in and ask for Frank Johnson.

FRANK JOHNSON

Harris waddles over to where I'm straightening a flatbed tire rim. The noise from the air drills and a semi backing in the shop is deafening so he has to yell to get my attention.

"Hey Frank!"

"Yeah?"

"Somebody up front to see you. What'd you ever do to get a slant-eyed looker come calling for you?"

"Don't know," I say. Stuff my gloves in my back pocket.

I weave through the scattered tools and tires to the reception area. Harris opens the door with a flourish, hitching up his britches, sucking in his gut. The looker stands in the middle of reception in a white blouse tight with a black bra clearly outlined beneath, miniskirt that gives out six inches above her knees, stiletto heels. Long black hair and sheeny mocha skin, sharp Asian features. Skinny but not flat-chested. Briefcase in hand and a smartphone in the other. I manage to look over her shoulder just long enough to see the blue car with state tags parked outside.

"This is him," says Harris. "Ole Frank."

She holds out a hand. "Good morning, Mr. Johnson. My name is Natty Elsinore."

"My hands are a little dirty, ma'am," I said, rubbing my palms on my coveralls.

"Good," she says.

I take her hand. It glows in mine, like soft sand on a postcard.

NATTY ELSINORE

I shut the break room door behind us, gesture for Frank Johnson to sit. The break room has a microwave and cracked shelves, table etched with obscenities, folding chairs and an ancient coffee machine. I set my briefcase and phone on the table and sit kitty corner to him, slowly folding my legs right where he can see them, watching him watch me do it. He takes in the sight like I'm going to be the last woman he sees for a while.

"How'd you come by a name like that?" he asks.

I laugh, tinkly, a little surprised he's so blunt. Ironic, considering, and I like that in him. "I was adopted," I say.

No doubt he's pondering the odds on running for it. A dangerous time to be in a room alone with him. I lean in, pushing out cleavage. His eyes flick down.

"Mr. Johnson. I am a Special Investigator with Wyoming Health and Human Services. Child Protective Services."

He doesn't say anything.

"Would you like to see my badge?"

"What for?"

"All right. I have a question for you."

"Shoot."

"Where are the Shamzid children?"

"Who?" he says.

Liars always have tics, little twitches you can pick up on. He hardly has any. He's good enough to fool any amateur out there. Well, he has had plenty of practice.

"Let's not begin our relationship with fabrications," I say, biting a bottom lip, drawing another involuntary eye flick.

"I don't know what you're talking about."

"Let me phrase it a little differently, then, see if that helps your comprehension. Where are the Shamzid children, Mr. Dacono?"

AXEL DACONO

Three years ago, I busted my little brother C.C. out of a VA facility.

Let me back up. Me and C.C. got separated when my daddy took off with C.C. in the ratty backseat of our Chevy Nova, ditching me and my mom at an interstate rest stop outside Coeur d'Alene. I was six. C.C. was four. Mama died three days later. OD'd in a camper we were squatting in, left me with dogs at the door.

What happened next was, I got sucked into group homes, foster families, food vouchers. I kept trying to find C.C. but no desk monkey sucking state teat had time for an orphaned kid with no papers and no lawyers. In the meantime I learned to fight and fix a car. Emancipated at eighteen, I headed down to the warm in Florida. I did all right. Got a job, took some classes at a community college, got married, quit taking classes, got divorced. Kept looking for C.C. all the while.

I finally found him at a VA home in Massachusetts, strapped to a wheelchair with a shirtfront drenched in drool on account of the shards of Iraqi shrapnel jiggling in his brain. Same bureaucratic bullshit: no amount of cajoling or common sense would convince the desk monkeys to release C.C. Dacono to me, his brother, Axel Dacono. Fill out this form, Mr. Dacono, he requires round-the-clock medical attention, Mr. Dacono, come back at two o'clock to see Mr. Dipshit, Mr. Dacono.

They did let me wheel him around the facility, though, and one day I wheeled him out to the parking lot, tucked him in the backseat and headed west, back roads all the way. Chugged into this little Wyoming town black smoke belching from the hood.

That's when I became Frank Johnson. Got a job at Powers's Tire Shop and rented a converted hunting cabin down by the North Platte River. Rigged up C.C.'s wheelchair with rubber tires to roll him out to the riverbank so he could keep me company fishing. Subscribed to a long feed of medical sites and learned how to order prescription drugs from Mexico. I keep C.C. free of bedsores, on a high vitamin diet, exercise his limbs to stave off atrophy, clean his shit, trim his beard. I'm a good nurse. Sometimes I think I ought to go into it.

We sat out there by the river in the sunshine and the snow and I talked. Told him how mama died, and everything that happened to me after. Took six months to get to the present. Now I detail my days to him, down to the last lug nut.

Also, I ask him questions. What happened to dad, how'd he get himself blown up in Iraq. He never answers. So I speak for him and if my story doesn't answer to the facts it is satisfying to me even so.

"I'm waiting," Natty Elsinore says.

"I don't know what you're talking about," I say.

She reaches into her briefcase for a file. "How about this? 'C.C. Dacono, US Army, Purple Heart winner. Abducted from the Great Leydan Veterans Administration facility while in a persistent vegetative state.' Ring any bells?" She sets the file down. "A decorated veteran, Mr. Dacono. Did you know that?"

"Every ijit who gets blown up over there gets hisself a medal."

"You know, it's possible a jury would be sympathetic to your story. Long-lost brothers reunited, etcetera etcetera. Maybe you'd only get seven to ten upstate. Maybe C.C. would still be hanging on when you got out. Hard to tell, given his condition. The doctors out in Massachusetts didn't think he'd last this long, did they? That a chance you're prepared to take? Right now, I mean? Because I'm primed to make some phone calls. My fingers get itchy around a touchscreen."

She spins her phone on the table, smiles with daggers and needles. I don't say anything.

"Let me ask you again, Mr. Dacono," she says. "Where are the Shamzid children?"

She smiles, leans back in the chair, fiddles with her skirt so that a long slice of thigh shows.

NATTY ELSINORE

I was orphaned in a Bangkok hospital. Before I was adopted by my mom and dad and brought to America, I lingered for thirteen months in a stifling hall with a hundred other mewling babies, staring at the water stains on the ceiling, flies treading on my eyes, half-starving, covered in boils. I remember. I swear I do.

Doctors have told me there are no lingering effects from my early malnutrition and host of tropical ailments, parasites, dysentery, and so on. Complete recovery, I'm as normal as normal can be.

Except I'm not. I never have got out of that hall. I spend my days with a singular obsession: keeping other children out of it. I don't do anything else. Don't drink, don't go out, never had a man who was more to me than a fuck buddy. Most nights I stay up with my files and some nights I go out and act on what I read in them. As in the Shamzid children.

"I don't know," says Axel Dacono, aka Frank Johnson.

"Care for me to recite the list of people who've seen you fishing with those children on the river, walking them home, bringing them groceries?" I ask. "Did you know little Ashtin Shamzid drew a picture of you in school? It's hanging in Mrs. Foster's classroom. Right on the bulletin board. Mrs. Foster who got out of Ashtin that his daddy had gone missing."

"What's me knowing them have anything to with that?"

"I was sort of hoping you'd tell me."

AXEL DACONO

I met the Shamzid children on a Saturday afternoon early last spring. I was rolling C.C. down along the riverside to the Deeps and there they were, two little boys and their big sister, fishing. They had fishing line, anyway, knotted to sticks. A laundry detergent box filled with dirt and worms. An empty Coke carton to flop fish in. A regular Norman Rockwell painting except it was about thirty-four degrees and sleeting. They weren't out for the fun of it. They were out for food.

"Any luck?" I said.

The three of them jumped like wild cats. The littlest boy dropped his pole in the water.

"Stupid," said the middle boy to him.

The littlest boy started to cry and for a second I thought he would jump in after it. Damn lucky he didn't. You go down in the Deeps, you ain't coming up. The Deeps are where water pools up behind sluice gate turbines. They say the turbines have churned up the riverbed to where they can't get a depth anymore. Monsters grow out there, twenty-five inch trout that weigh in at twenty pounds, carp big enough to swallow a Labrador.

"No one said we couldn't be here," said the little girl, edging away, reaching for the littlest boy's hand.

"It's state land," I said. "Anyone can be here."

"We seen you down here before," said the middle boy.

"Hope I was having better luck than you." I looked at that stick fishing pole swirling in the Deeps. "Course, some luck you got to make yourself."

I took one of my poles from the tube on the back of C.C.'s wheelchair, loosened the line, went over to the little boy, lure jangling. "Now here's a rig you can catch you some fish with," I said.

"Really?" he said, not reaching for the pole.

"You bet. Just stay back from the bank."

The kid took the pole and you know what, he didn't cast too bad, hitting open water on the first go.

"Lemme try," said his older brother, dropping his stick.

"Lyle!" said the girl. "Let him do it."

Lyle stood by his little brother, pouting, while the little boy reeled in. God, but I wanted something to strike but the world ain't got much magic of that sort.

The girl looked at C.C. lolling in the wheelchair. "What's the matter with him?" she asked.

"Bad government," I said. "The other two of you got names?"

"I'm G'ewel," she said, brushing sleet off C.C.'s shoulders. "My other brother there is Ashtin."

Come to find out, that's how their daddy named them, spelling and all. You hardly need to know much more about the man than that. I got out the other pole, handed it to Lyle. "You live up in East Jane?"

"Yeah," said G'ewel. "Every day."

We took to meeting regular down at the river after that. They started coming over to the house to fry up what we caught. Went against all my principles of hiding out, but they didn't know the first thing about nothing, not to how to tell the tail from the guts or how operate a frying pan. By the time they learned, I got to where I missed them when they weren't around.

"I don't got what you're looking for," I say to Ms. Elsinore.

"If that line of conversation's not to your taste, Mr. Dacono," she says, "let's change the subject."

I wish I had the Persuader on me. Most times all you got to do is snick the expandable baton out to full length and you get your way, but I doubt this Natty Elsinore is the type to back off. I picture her on the floor spasming after I crack her in the temple, shitting her pretty panties, drooling. Me strolling past Harris at the counter then going hell-bent for leather home for C.C. and the open road. I've pictured variations on that scene a million times or more, every time a stranger calls my name, every time I pass a cop cruiser.

Except. It ain't just me and C.C. any more. There's them kids and Jade to consider.

NATTY ELSINORE

Best thing my daddy ever did for me was teach me to hunt. "Tiny as you are, girl," he used to say, "you ought to be able to knife a sparrow in a popcorn field." I almost can. So investigating that river bottom where Axel Dacono lives and fishes was like a stroll through the mall for me.

I have seen him with the Shamzid kids fishing at the Deeps in the bright morning sun. And in the afternoon when he gets home from work with hugs and root beer and late at night when they're asleep, walking the house with that man named Jerry. And I have watched those children, with him. They are not afraid. They are not ill-treated. They may be better off than they have ever been in their lives. I know Jerry is better off for knowing Axel Dacono. His hospital release papers were co-signed by one Mr. Frank Johnson.

Yes, they have a kind of togetherness, that odd group. Family-like, you could say. I almost envy them.

"Let's talk about our mutual friend Terl Shamzid," I say. "What happens when he comes home?"

"You know where he is?"

"I know where he was. And I can make a good guess as to when he'll get here."

Axel Dacono shrugs. A very unconvincing show of indifference.

"I have looked into the files on the Shamzid kids, you know. No kin of record, no one to contact, nothing. You know those forms parents have to fill out for their kids at school? You know what their daddy Terl put down for emergency contact number?"

"What?"

"911."

Axel snorts. "Where'd he go?"

"Does it matter? He abandoned his children for eleven days. Twelve tomorrow. Of course, his being gone hasn't been all bad, has it? They're out of East Jane, right?"

AXEL DACONO

East Jane Valley is the trailer park up the river past the Deeps. The kind of country ghetto you ain't going to read about in your newsfeed, water heaters ripped out of broken-down trailers to lie in the weeds, local yokels breaking down doors for meth busts while twacked-out tweakers sprawled on plywood stoops watch. The school bus only stops on the county road, the driver won't pull into East Jane itself, no, sir, a ten-second stop for what kids will come and then no slowing down till he hits the respectable farm houses down the road.

It's been home for the Shamzid kids for nearly a year, living on stick jerky, candy bars and Coke, when their daddy remembered that much. They all had perfect school attendance because of the hot lunch. Their daddy didn't work, couldn't abide anyone's talk but his own, barely seemed to know their names. G'ewel told me he'd been this way since their mamma died. Seemed like she remembered a house and a pink bedroom and a Christmas tree, but that could have just been TV shows.

Before he left, Terl Shamzid pulled up his daughter's shirt for a look and said she was about old enough to start earning her keep. Easy work, he told her. You just got to lay there.

Jade lives in the trailer across from them. He told me they showed up on Thanksgiving weekend last year.

"Looking like half-drowned puppies," Jade said. "I wanted to take them a turkey."

"Why didn't you?" I asked.

Jade ran a finger over the ragged scar etched above his left eye. "Didn't know what kind of man their daddy was."

Jade's real name is Jerry, but he won't answer to that. Two years ago he got jumped outside the Dollar Store in miniskirt and makeup. They dumped him out in the country when they were done with him. How we got to know one another was, I spotted him dragging himself out of the ditch bank. After he got out of the hospital I brought him over food till he could walk again. Kept telling him this was Wyoming, goddammit, not Miami Beach, and next time they might not stop at baseball bats.

Since then he comes over a couple times a week. He's a good cook, doesn't change my station on the radio, likes fish. The deal we have is, Jade keeps his mouth shut about C.C., and he doesn't go out in public dressed like a woman any more. No, he saves the prancing in frills and panties and lace for my house. I came up in boys' homes and foster families. I don't mind a man.

Now he's staying out at my place, too. I commissioned him to look after the kids. He takes them out to the school bus stop, picks them up. Makes sure they get to school, have milk in the fridge. He's convinced G'ewel she's pretty, especially when he does her hair, and keeps telling Ashtin and Lyle what super smart little hunks they are. I've no doubt it's the first time anyone has ever preened over those kids in their lives.

I shift in my chair again. All the obligations. I can't run.

"Look," says Ms. Elsinore. "I don't need to tell you what'll happen to those children when the state takes them. The foster homes, the group therapy. The separations."

"No. You don't got to tell me."

"Mr. Dacono, let us yank on the brass balls of this thing. What do you say?"

What could I say?

NATTY ELSINORE

This Axel Dacono isn't really a hard one. That's why he rescued his brother, that transsexual, those kids. You might even go so far as to say he's morally upright. Better yet, he's amenable to straight talk. He runs a tongue over his teeth. He isn't glancing anywhere near my legs sheeny in the overhead fluorescent light. Someone pokes his head in the break room, cussing kindly at the closed door, coffee mug in hand. Sees us in there, excuses himself, and closes the door.

"Here's what I can offer you, Mr. Dacono," I say. "Legitimacy. Genuine and uncut. Your ID profile's a little shaky at the moment, wouldn't you say? It wasn't that hard to dig you out. I'm just the first one to take enough interest in you to do it. And now the subterfuge is over. You aren't hiding out any more. You're found. That part you got, right?"

"It's why I'm still sitting here."

"Good. So tell me. How would you feel about becoming the state-appointed guardian of the Shamzid children?"

He shifts in his chair. "I ain't confessing nothing," he says.

"Quite the contrary, Mr. Dacono. Being a state-appointed guardian legitimizes your profile. From then on a background check runs in that direction, you see, rather than ... well, rather than in the direction I ran it. The paperwork shuffles your way for once. Axel Dacono, he's gone." I snap my fingers. "You're Frank Johnson."

He leans forward, toys with a spare pencil on the table. "What about their daddy?"

I smile, lean forward so that my collarbones just and my bra straps show under the bulge of my shirt, a move I have practiced many times in front of the mirror. He doesn't even glance.

"It all hinges on our mutual friend," I say.

AXEL DACONO

I get back to the shop floor as Harris looks watches Natty Elsinore's ass toggle out the door. All afternoon, working on tires, greasing up equipment, sweeping floors, I think about Terl Shamzid. I have already thought about him a great deal. Through long nights, watching the kids sleep, little mouths hung open, hair rumpled, tiny fingers curled on the floorboards, I have thought and thought about him.

After work I stop by Walmart for ground beef and root beer. Furtive in and out of there like always. Fill my basket, express checkout. I watch the families checking out with carts piled high, playing peek-a-boo with babies, idly thumbing glossy magazines. Not a thought in the world that they're one thumbprint away from the end of everything, like me.

I drive home five miles under the limit, seat belt securely fastened, radio at a reasonable volume. Pull into my yard in the slanted late afternoon sun. The kids have rolled C.C. down to the riverside. G'ewel is combing out his hair. Ashtin is sitting on my fishing chair, struggling with an orange. Lyle has the Persuader. He's practicing snicking it out and pushing it back in. On the old wire spool there are a couple gutted trout. With a real pole, he's gotten to be a decent little fisherman. I stand at the edge of the trees a minute, watching.

G'ewel waves. I walk over. These kids don't say hello, just like they don't say goodbye. They've learned to measure their words, every syllable. Jade comes out of the house, wearing cut-off jean shorts and a T-shirt three sizes too small for him. Ashtin runs over for a hug. I put him up on my shoulders and run loops around the yard and when I look over at C.C. slumped in his wheelchair I swear he smiles. Then it's gone, and he's a mound of meat stuck in a chair again. I lower Ashtin off my shoulders and he hands me his orange.

"This time I'm going to get it," I say.

"Huh-uh," says Ashtin, shaking his head, grinning.

"You watch. I'm feeling lucky."

"You say that every day."

I peel carefully. In a week I haven't gotten one off in one go yet. I believe Ashtin's losing faith in me. And yet again the rind drops to the ground before I get there.

"You can't win em all," I say, and shuck the rest of the peel and hand the orange to Ashtin. "You read them library books?"

"No," says Ashtin.

"You, Lyle?" I say.

"I guess," says Lyle, handing me The Persuader.

"You guess or you did?"

"I tried. But I don't get em."

"That's why you have to keep at it, then. It'll come. You got to read stuff. Well, what about them magazines, G'ewel?"

"They're okay," says G'ewel. "Lots of pretty girls."

"Pretty like you," says Jade.

I get up and strut around like a supermodel with Jade. Lyle and Ashtin laugh and G'ewel smiles, a little. Progress. I scoop Ashtin up. Twirl and swing him around as he brays with laughter. Then he is gurgling and grabbing for his neck. G'ewel yelps and I jam fingers down his throat, yank out a wad of orange pulp. He gags and throws up all over me and then sits there spluttering, G'ewel pounding his back. I put my arms around the lot of them.

"There, there," I say. "There, there."

NATTY ELSINORE

My phone rings at half past midnight. It's Axel. I'm in bed, looking at some photographs. Other cases, other kids, a lot less hope.

"I talk to C.C. sometimes," he says. "Tell him everything. I think he understands. You know?"

"Yes," I say, chewing my lip, because I would like to know such a thing very much. Someone of your own blood to talk to. What I would give.

"Is it true?" he says. "What you told me?"

"Yes. Those kids will be placed in your custody. You have my word."

AXEL DACONO

I am sitting in Terl Shamzid's trailer. Past one in the morning. Terl Shamzid is on his way. Natty has been following him, texting me on his progress.

The kids are home, asleep. Jade texted me the whole evening's progression: the kids are eating dinner, the kids are watching TV, the kids are fussing around getting into jammies, the kids are asleep.

The car pulls up outside, the headlights blink off. The man comes in. He sees me standing by his chair past the kitchenette. He doesn't seem surprised and rummages through the shelf, pulls out a yellow plastic cup, runs it under the tap, drinks it off.

"And who the fuck are you?" he says, droplets glimmering in his whiskers.

"Doesn't matter," I say.

Terl looks at me. Scratches his thigh. Sets the yellow cup down on the cracked counter. "Well, I ain't got nothing for you. Get in line, cocksucker."

"Aren't you going to ask where your kids are?"

"Goddamn foster home, probably."

"Guess again," I say, and snick out the Persuader.

NATTY ELSINORE

I stand by the river with Frank Johnson, looking out on the Deeps. First cold night of the year and our breath makes little white stabs into the darkness. I don't know what we're watching for. Terl Shamzid isn't coming up. Ever.

"Now what?" Frank Johnson asks.

I shrug. "Paperwork," I say. "My end of the deal. You're going to like having a family."

"I like it already," he says.

FRANK JOHNSON

Three weeks later. Snowy November day. We pile out of the car, me, G'ewel, Ashtin, Lyle, Jade. I hold C.C. while Jade and G'ewel unfold the wheelchair from the trunk. Set him down gently and let Lyle push him. Lyle likes to have jobs. I hold Ashtin's hand. Jade holds G'ewel's.

Together we walk across the blacktop, towards that shining Walmart facade.

A STRAIGHT FACE

หนี

Mekk didn't want to marry Nit. He didn't have anything against her. But he wanted out of the sticks, out of Chang Saen, on the road, down to Bangkok, out where he could make his own name. Here in Chang Saen he would someday run his father's grocery, making him the grocer. Right now he was Nit's Fiancé. In ten minutes he'd be at the district office and he'd sign the papers and then he would be Nit's Husband.

He was sitting on his puttering motorbike with Nit behind him, waiting for the light to change at the market intersection. She kept wanting to put her arms around him, but he shrugged her off. Other motorbikes were running the red light, swerving through the slow-moving cross traffic, but he stayed put.

"We are rock-solid," Mekk's father said. "People will always buy vegetables and toothpaste and ice and Coke."

Mekk nodded, and kept at the drudgery around the grocery, stacking goods, counting change. Sometimes, though, he got to make a trip to loading docks for supplies. He lingered in the shade of the jackfruit trees with the truck drivers, drinking rice whiskey. Pretended he was one of them, bound for a road anywhere. He used his pocket money to keep the whiskey flowing, to keep their stories flowing. Bedding a girl on a stack of rice sacks, fisticuffs with a rival syndicate's truckers on a Bangkok wharf, saline pools shimmering with blue electric light as a lightning storm crashing across the salt farms, gunning away from a gang of insurgents on a lonely mountain road down south.

He returned to the grocery with booze reeking from his pores to find Nit had been waiting on him for hours. She sat demurely on a stack of rice sacks, not meeting his eyes. He wanted to fuck her right there but had barely completed the thought before his father cuffed him and shoved him into a storeroom.

Mekk shielded himself from more blows, but they did not come. His father sighed.

"No more, boy," he said. "Learn your place. This grocery will fall apart without constant care, same as a man without a wife. Nit is the perfect bride. All else will grow in time. Do you understand me?"

"Yes," said Mekk.

Mekk understood, all right. What could you say against Nit? She really was everything everyone said, lovely and gentle and smooth-natured, of good name and repute. In her quiet way, Nit loved him. Mekk knew that much. After this became a generally agreed-upon fact, they didn't talk about it. They didn't much talk about anything, sitting across from each other at endless meals in restaurants where she ate whatever he ordered. He didn't even know what her favorite food was. She had replicas of Pooh Bear and Doraemon attached to her phone, and he didn't know why, or which she liked better. They sat in theaters, primly not holding hands like the other bantering couples, waiting for the movie to start.

One time he brought her to the rock outcropping just off the highway overlooking the reservoir, his favorite spot in the whole world that he knew of, so far. He thought the beauty of the overlook would provoke some feeling, in him, in her, but it didn't. Nit had nothing much to say, then as on any other time. She was content to be wherever he was, like a cat that only purrs in the presence of one person.

"What if we made a run for it?" he said.

What are you talking about?" Nit said. "Run where?"

"To Bangkok! Start up a whole new life."

"What?" she said.

"Never mind," he said, hurling a rock into the water. "Will you be happy running a grocery with me till forever?"

"Forever," Nit said.

Mekk was pretty sure that was the only word she heard. Come to think of it, it was the only one he'd heard, too. What would they say to each other for all the coming years? He in his place, she in hers. The Grocer. Forever the Grocer. Sure, everyone knew the only love that lasted was the kind that started off at a slow burn. But he was already burning fast, there at the market stoplight in the exhaust fumes.

He twisted on the accelerator and Nit almost fell off the back of the bike.

"Where are we going?" she shouted.

But he pretended he didn't hear through his helmet, the silver one with the shiny opaque facemask. He liked wearing this helmet on. He liked to smirk at the town from behind it. Without the helmet, he always had to keep a straight face.

Mekk swerved through the traffic, away from the District Office, out of town. He didn't look back or slow down. They burst into the green of the countryside, swooping past the overflowing sugarcane fields and the stilted huts where poor farmers and old people lived, whining around slow-moving trucks belching black fumes on the winding road. Nit held on to him tight, trusting, plaited hair flapping in the wind, head between his shoulder blades. Sure, he was supposed to be marrying her right now, but right now he had the helmet and she didn't.

Ahead was the reservoir and the road jogged sharply right around the outcropping that jutted into the road. He twisted back the accelerator far as it would go. Rocks looming big in his facemask, he grinned and leaned the bike over hard left.

WE WOULD START HERE

ล่มสลาย

En had a thing about photos. True, she had all kinds of superstitious hang-ups. Mirrors and colors and candles and etcetera. But she made a special point about photos. She said you could never leave them behind. Intact pictures were unguarded portals to your soul. She mentioned this after she put a couple pictures of us on the TV. It was like she expected to leave, to have to leave. I sometimes saw her looking at them wistfully, as though they were already gone.

Not that she took everything so seriously. For instance, next to those sacred pictures she carefully placed animal bobbleheads. These she got from cereal boxes – a moose, a squirrel, a polar bear. She didn't much care for cereal, but she loved the bobbleheads. Many mornings in a row I went without the eggs and toast I'd taught her to make and she got nine or ten bobbleheads up there. I didn't mind. I'd have eaten banana slug sushi if it made her happy. When I finished up a box, she'd have a new one, emptied of bobblehead, ready the next morning.

Around then is when we both took to eating cereal at night, too. It was not that we loved cereal as much as all that. But those were the days when the stories began filtering in from the hinterlands on the backs of staggering survivors. The pandemic was spreading upcountry, worse than the worst conjectures of the most grim of doomsayers, but it wasn't until it was far too late that the full gravity of the situation was appreciated. Then a vaccination center (useless, since there was no vaccination) inexplicably appeared, and the gates burst. Our quaint town, home to the university where I was paid a ridiculously high salary to quote long lines of Shakespeare and Keats and Ginsberg to students mostly unable to comprehend Seuss, became a seething slum overnight. Never mind that we were hundreds of kilometers from the outbreak zones deep in muggy rice country. Where En was from.

We nonetheless remained chockfull of bravado. No one anywhere yet believed or accepted the outbreak could be as devastatingly biblical as it fast became. Home, reputedly safe and serene across the waters, crossed my mind. En, however, lacked a passport, or any official papers whatever. Moreover, she grew daily more worried for the fate of her upcountry village and would not have abandoned her homeland. But she wouldn't leave without me, and I wouldn't go anywhere without her.

In the early going, the university still paid my salary and the air-conditioned supermarket where we bought cereal, owned by a multinational both image-conscious and profit-hungry, remained open. We were there often in those days. With all the newcomers, food that wasn't prepackaged was an unknown quantity. Not everyone in town, after all, was a penniless beggar. Plenty found the moldering pepper-packed tidbits of dubious origin that passed for food among the peasants as unpalatable and potentially toxic as I did, and were equally willing to pay the premium for properly packaged foodstuffs. But then came the quarantine. The managers of the superstore, out of touch with their bosses across the ocean, were not above massive price gouging as the shelves emptied. The last box we managed to acquire cost nearly fifty times the normal price.

From our balcony overlooking the sea, filthy with floating turds and plastic sacks and castoff shirts and sandals, we watched the helicopters come. They hovered over town authoritative as scripture, blaring massively-decibeled bilingual announcements that foreign nationals would be evacuated on that day and that day only. The pronouncement warned that only bona fide foreigners with proper documentation would be allowed on the helicopters; the King's Own Guard had shoot-to-kill orders for any natives who attempted to contravene this directive. Foreigners had until sunset. We watched the helicopters thud over town, clutching each other as the sun started downward.

—§—

I met En some months previously. I was on a motorcycle tour upcountry on semester break, crossing the sprawling rice-plains on uncharted back roads. My ninth day out, a blinding rainstorm materialized. I rounded a slick bend too fast and there was a buffalo calmly working over its cud in the middle of the road. The dumb animal neither blinked nor moved as I smashed into it and flipped into a muddy ditch. My helmet prevented my head from splitting open, but several of my bones were not so fortunate. A peasant sheltering under a nearby banyan tree witnessed the incident. After ascertaining I was alive, he left me on the roadside to arrange transportation to a clinic some kilometers away. There, a quaking young doctor fixed me up as best he could and one of the clinic's three rooms was vacated for me. I remember only a soupy haze and strong brown hands that seemed constantly to be supporting my battered frame, and rain so heavy I fancied I was underwater.

The clinic had an endless supply of very strong painkillers: the superstitious peasants are great poppers of pills, of whose seemingly magical qualities they greatly approve. Thus I remained in a feeble state of intoxicated semi-consciousness. All the while it rained. Understanding only the rudiments of the vernacular and nothing of the rapidly twilling local dialect, attempts at communication were tortuous. The young doctor and his nurse, utterly unsure of what to do with the wounded foreigner in their midst, opted to do nothing.

On the third day it was made clear to me that floodwaters would soon swamp the clinic. The bridge to the main highway and hospitals and airports and home was already washed out. The young peasant who'd arranged my transportation reappeared. It turned out my motorcycle was being kept in his village. Also, the buffalo was dead. Also, his village, very near the scene of the accident, was on high ground. The panicky doctor placed me in his care, quickly rattling off a series of instructions I'm not sure the young peasant could follow. I was presented with my fully intact wallet and passport. Then we were off, in the back of a pickup with a tarp rigged over it, as I assured the doctor I would be most generous in repayment of his services. The nurse made me as comfortable as she could, propping me on cushions damp in the misty air, raindrops big as bullets pounding out a ceaseless staccato on the tarp.

Doped up as I was, I found the ride pleasant, enormous drops from the leaky tarp tapping my forehead, running down the bridge of my nose, tickling down my chest. At one point there was a great deal of slooshing water and frantic yelling. I learned later that a creek had turned into a washing torrent which reached the doors of the pickup and the young peasant, trailing us on a motorbike, was carried off. He survived, but his motorbike was never found. The road washed out minutes after we passed. When we reached the village, I was conveyed by means of a crude rope-and-pulley device up to a snug and wide room atop a stilted teak house, safe from the water that flowed around on all sides. I was deposited on a soft pallet, and was soon sucking sweet orange tea through a straw, which was served by a deep-brown, wide-smiling girl, who knelt next to the pallet and observed my every swallow.

I was in the house of the man whose buffalo I had so unceremoniously vanquished and whose son had nearly drowned. His family of nine talked and cooked and slept in that one room. They rightly thought I would be unable to tolerate such living conditions. So they decamped to various houses around the village, leaving the girl to look after me. En.

She was 19. Before her mother's death brought her back to the village at 15, she attended a year of Catholic boarding school in the provincial capital, where the charitable Sisters of Mercy taught her her halting English. But everything you needed to know about her you got by watching. She was suffused with gentle life and soft-eyed wonder. She knew almost nothing, but was rich in the inherited wisdom of a hundred generations of mud-tilling peasantry. For me she had an earthy reverence no citified girl anywhere in the world could match. She lavished on me the assiduous care of a doting mother, shy new bride, and dutiful daughter.

The family buffalo, while it still existed, was kept underneath the house. This accounted for the rank bovine reek that stalked my feverish dreams the first few nights, herds of fire-breathing bison bent on revenge. Awake I remained in my drugged haze, unremitting rain on the tin roof above. En kept a small fire going and over it produced rice and broth dishes from a few unlikely-looking sacks in the corner, delicious even to my jaundiced taste buds. My depth perception unbalanced and my motor control shaky, she ladled food into my mouth, my innocent-intentioned hand resting on a soft thigh. After I finished, she ate soundlessly with her hands, obsidian-pupiled eyes glistening as a slight smile curved into her high-boned cheek. She gave me a yellow-spiced soup which soothed my throat and long-stemmed leaves which had the miraculous effect of causing the itching inside the casts on my right shoulder and left foot to disappear. She dried my clothes by the fire. They came back smoke-smelling but precisely folded. She attended to my bathroom needs deftly and with no expressed embarrassment. She was never more than 10 feet away and never had her back turned for more than a few seconds. She hummed tunes whose gentle warblings modulated into my brain while stroking my forehead by the hour.

Below came alarming rustling and shrieks and hissings. The creatures of the forest sought high ground. En executed several snakes and scorpions, and clubbed away a furry raccoon-looking creature that clambered up the ladder. She hauled the ladder up and set bitter incense sticks in the corners. We were cut off from the world while the storm pelted on

There were no windows in the room and not much to look at. Faintly visible in the wet half-light was a small Buddhist altar in the corner, a portrait of the King and Queen smiling benevolently down, and a couple blue-faded pictures from an old tire calendar. So I passed the hours peering into her face, memorizing every contour and pore and shade. At nights a chill settled in. En crawled onto the pallet next to me, pulled a blanket over us and rested her head in the crook of my shoulder, my arm resting lightly on her. She was a little furnace, chasing the chill back into the dark. Though aroused by the soft press of her belly and breasts, I was as comfortable as if I lay in a palace, and every night I soon drifted off to sleep.

The rain stopped. Within minutes, the clouds broke and sunlight poured over the saturated land. I watched it march yellow across the floor from the entranceway. Everywhere the gaping chinks of the walls were shiny stripes. The light melted the cobwebs in my brain. Not only the light – my supply of drugs was gone. It had been one week since my accident.

By the heat of the afternoon, I was ready to get out of the room. My body ached mercilessly, but sobriety impelled me forward. Leaning on En and hopping unsteadily on one leg, I made it to the entranceway, where I sat and dangled my legs over the edge. Word spread and what seemed the entire village turned out to see my appearance. Protective En refused to let me attempt getting down on my own. The young peasant, whose name was Ni and who was En's brother, came to the rescue, hoisting me on his back and piggybacking me down. Once there, ground foggy with evaporating damp, sky so crystalline clouds seemed an impossible illusion, it was obvious someone would have to be continuously at my side. At a grunt from En's father, squatting and smoking under the shade of the house in his empty pen, En got the job. I was relieved. Ni had a rough grip and unpleasant scent. Besides, I already needed En like a lifeline.

The two of us wandered the village, me leaning heavily on her and using a cane Ni had fashioned out of bamboo, surrounded by a dozen dirty-faced children and almost as many mangy dogs. The village sat on a rise overlooking the rice-plains, now a vast expanse of silver-sheened water. It consisted of around 20 houses, all wisely stilted off the ground, and a few structures for silkworms and silk, weaved by the village women. There were a couple tiny sundry shops, tissues and toothbrushes and hard candy and rice whisky on offer. On the village road were silent-passing refugees headed back to the low-lying areas, towing children and handcarts. As we watched, the dogs stopped barking and retreated whimpering to the shadows and the children fell silent. Most had lost everything they did not carry. The women and children were grim-faced and the men looked hungover. En told me they were. Nothing left but to drink.

She took me to the empty shed where my motorcycle was. The thing was trashed: shattered headlight festooned with bloody tufts of stiff black hair, handlebars and forks bent in, long streaks of bare chrome, blinker brackets crunched sideways, speedometer cracked open. Just looking at the thing gave me icy trembles and visions of fiery screaming crashes, crunching metal and bone. Leaning heavily on stoic 100-pound En, I turned away. Not a chance I could get on the thing again. I'd have to get out of town another way. Though with En next to me, I felt no especial hurry. We walked on.

Weak and bruised and aching, I think I was never so happy as in that backwater with nothing but time and her, limping around a world as lush and luminous and Edenic as any the explorers knew. En was more lovely by the day and was close to me every night. Chewing on long-stemmed leaf with her next to me on the pallet, memories of what it was to sleep alone drained away. As her heat rose next to me I once stroked the back of her neck, but that was as far as it went. I depended too much on her to risk anything, no matter how my heart pounded. She gave me no hints. We were chaste as children.

The village was besieged with green undergrowth that everywhere threatened to snag my clumsy feet. Garish green creeping tendrils, grasping creepers outfitted with thorns, sickly-sweet scented orange flowers whose wispish stems belied a hardy elasticity that easily tripped up a handicapped pedestrian: they abruptly appeared with the sickly verdure of tropical life. We made an excursion to some rice paddies nearby, down a narrow trail through a banyan grove, laughing uproariously at my shaky attempts to stay upright. Hunched-over workers knee-deep in mud stared as if we were an alien race. I saw that with me, En was no longer one of them. I began to grasp at my responsibilities.

The doctor took a break from overseeing repairs to his mud-encrusted clinic and came to the village. He arrived with the nurse. She had a saw. The X-ray machine at his clinic was destroyed, the doctor said, but in a few days, maybe a week, the bridge would be repaired and it would be possible to reach the provincial capital, where he supposed hospitals still functioned. However, in his professional opinion, based on his memory of my X-rays, my breaks were sufficiently healed by now. If the casts came off, he said, I would require at least two weeks recuperation here. I looked at En. The casts came off.

Nearly a month of sweat and grit made the stench intense. The skin beneath was a splotchy purple which, I was assured, looked much worse than it was. My foot could take no weight and my shoulder couldn't support so much as an empty backpack, but they seemed functional. More important, I still had them. More important yet, I had En. The doctor, sweating mightily in the close room, asked how I felt. Never better, I said.

Communications reopened. The village phone was placed in my service and I reluctantly placed calls to the university and family back in the US, the former laconically beginning to note my absence, the latter frantic with worry. I soothed my family, in particular my elderly mother, who'd been pestering the embassy daily, explaining that in this part of the world it was indeed possible for a flood to cut off communication and transport for weeks at a time. I was all but ordered to return to civilization, causing me to spend most of the call deflecting innuendo. In light of the hysteria, I didn't get around to mentioning the accident or my injuries or En.

Leaving the village was definitely on my mind. Each day came a keening fear of a future alone. This was no imaginary demon. I knew all about the solitary life. And now here was En, so perfectly kind that it seemed a perfect folly to ever be without her. One blazing afternoon alone in our room, I said as much.

She agreed with a few deep nods – indicators of deep

excitement. Her father, I thought, would not be so thrilled. I contrived an excuse: I wished to formally repay En's family for their unstinting hospitality in cash and coastal goods, with En to serve as delivery girl. Once with me, En would not leave, and I hoped her father would have no choice but to accept our fait accompli. To demonstrate my good character, I bequeathed my motorcycle to Ni. Who had already begun repairs with such tools as he had and, by all accounts, was making a remarkable success of the job. I didn't doubt that his havenot resourcefulness would have it like new in no time. Ni reacted to the gift with a quick smile and immediately jogged off to continue work on his new possession. En's father remained behind. With En as my soft-voiced interpreter, I made my case in that overhead room.

At first I thought her father's clipped response was disgust or dismissal. I launched in on an arsenal of secondary arguments. But En shook her head and placed a small palm on my arm, just as she did to steady my wobbly walking. Do not worry, she told me. He understands. I will go with you.

I realized En had not translated at all. She made her own case. I did not care. It wasn't for me to question the universe in a bountiful mood. Meanwhile, I was informed a university vehicle was en route to ferry me home. The staffer with whom I spoke seemed somewhat bewildered at my being so far away to begin with. It would arrive in three days.

There were some details to sort out. To begin with, in view of the great generosity of En's family, coupled with the loss of her labor, it was agreed I would send a monthly remuneration to her family. I readily agreed to the paltry requested sum. I felt as soft Westerners of my type do, that it was beneath my dignity to quibble over money. For her father's part, he seemed almost miffed I didn't deign to bargain.

I was at great pains to make it clear to all and sundry that En was to me no mere maid, that my feelings were of a far more intimate nature. Evidently this confirmed the general village belief that, as we shared sleeping quarters, we were betrothed. It was therefore necessary to cement our bond, as well as En's new status as the chosen one of a (relatively speaking) rich (if foolish and foreign) man. One evening, the whole of the village, starting with the monks and her father and ending with tiny children, lined up to tie a white string around each of our wrists. Incense wisped around us as a coterie of old men kept up a steady chant. Half my forearm was covered in white string and I learned that in the eyes of the village, we were now officially engaged. En told me it didn't really mean anything, but I saw by the soft turn of her head she didn't believe this herself. Neither did I. Nor did I want to.

Then there was En's leaving ceremony. It seemed as though every female in the village had something to contribute – bits of silk, hairpins, silver-coated cups, all specially deemed to be bringers of good fortune. I sat behind En as the women came. En showed me every item as the giver watched, and I conferred upon each a beneficent nod. Also, it was necessary to consult the village medium. She was a small woman dressed in a white gown that resembled pajamas and was soiled at the heels. She twitched in a trance, clutching a statue of the Elephant God and muttering incantations in a voice resembling a coal miner with a two-pack-a-day habit. She closely examined our palms, rubbing gold leaf on mine and making prints of En's on a square of raw yellow silk with the blood of some creature. She spoke in the deepest dialect and I understood nothing. After, En told me with great relief that the medium had foreseen a long happy future, so long as we avoided malevolent water spirits. I decided not to mention that my apartment overlooked the sea. After the medium returned to her rather mousy normal state, En's father placed a fistful of bills in her hand. I concluded you get the news you pay for.

My last night in the village, it was de rigueur I be with the menfolk, drinking rotgut rice whisky around the fire. The men asked a few polite questions, the same ones I'd been asked seventy dozen times since I'd been in the country: where was I from, how old was I, what did I do, did I like the food, was it too spicy for me. They seemed satisfied with my pat answers. Of course, they weren't really interested. Not with the serious business of drinking at hand. The talk quickly went beyond my comprehension and lasted half the night. Out of boredom, I kept on drinking. Whenever I picked up a glass, my compadres began chanting and I was required to down its entire contents, which were immediately replenished. There was also all manner of food, chunky and chewy and crunchy, whose vaguely nonvertebrae origins I did not dare hazard a guess at. But to be polite, I turned down nothing.

Owing to the poor condition of the roads, the university vehicle arrived half a day late. Not that I was aware of it. I was dead to the world, having passed out without coming to know my putative fiancée on any more intimate terms, despite my intentions and the bleated-out cries of encouragement from my erstwhile drinking buddies as I wobbled away from the party. En stroked my forehead gently as I woke. Those first few bleary moments of consciousness with only her in my vision did not linger nearly long enough. I stood up shakily. Below were a couple befuddled representatives from the university, somewhat scandalized to find the celebrated professor reduced to such primitive straits.

They did not quite believe En was coming along. My words to the effect on the phone had been politely disregarded as the ravings of an injured man. How could the prized professor bring himself so low – this coarse peasant was unfit, probably, to sweep the hallways of their sacred institution. The representatives milled around as though I had proposed a suicide assault on the royal citadel. Clearly they wanted to consult their superiors, but could not without being so inexcusably rude as to publicly question my judgment. En hovered behind my left shoulder, eyes downcast and saying nothing, her presence undeniably real as she followed the proceedings. The representatives were somewhat softened to learn En was my fiancée, though this also bewildered them further. Also it created a catch in my throat as I mouthed the words for the first time. In the end, they concluded there was no accounting for the strange ways of foreigners, and on this provisional basis accepted her presence. They loaded up our possessions, which fit into two small bags, and had been mostly acquired in the preceding three days.

I expected (and hoped for) a great sendoff from the villagers in whose presence my life had so greatly metamorphosed. I did not receive one. En's grandmother waved feebly from the doorway of a shack, and that was all. No one there believed in goodbye. Then we were out on the highway, lined with debris encrusted in dried mud, finely moted dust hazing out the late afternoon sun. The countryside was an alluvial plain, ownership and property and division blotted out by flat mud deposits. Everywhere peasants labored to return the country to its former condition. I could see they would be at their work a long time and might never succeed entirely. I pulled En close, happy to have spared her their sisyphean labors.

—§—

Back in the coastal town, we at last consummated what had been nearly two months in the making. After, we fell asleep with the ease of longtime lovers, her warm body a shield from the terrors of the night. We did not leave the bed until the following afternoon. We did not leave the apartment for days. I reshaped my former views of an indifferent universe and the inevitability of suffering. Her placid ways smoothed over the rough edges of my life in that hot country, and soon all the time before her seemed a pointless struggle.

Only one thing grated, and then only briefly: En was no virgin. That she was already despoiled must have been general village knowledge. Surely her father would never have placed his daughter alone for nights on end with a strange foreigner, even an injured one, had she still purity to preserve. Several times I began to question around the edges of her history. En evaded my inquisitions with such gentle alacrity that I cheerfully gave up. She was in my blood and no remote history could change that. My rather palatial suite nineteen stories above the sea became a snug home. If En remembered the medium's prognostication, she didn't mention it. And if the university mucky-mucks had anything to say about my live-in, they didn't do it in my presence.

In the village En was so thin she had angles. With access to all the food her stomach desired, she rounded out. She insisted on cooking and daily prepared more food than we could eat in two settings. Nor did she shy away from fatty, sugar-laden western food, developing a taste for steak and cheese and pasta ladled over in thick sauces. Her skin shone and the doctor said she was as lustily healthy as any human being had the right to expect. She didn't much care about the suite's view or the spectacular sunsets, but she delighted in the elevator and the remote control and hailing taxis.

I enrolled her in English classes at the university, with a view to the eventual completion of her education. We went to a market to get a book bag for her. She took great care in selecting it, asking me over and over if I was sure about the dimensions of the textbooks. Rank food stalls with upcountry fare had appeared, which En leaped at the chance to patronize, and beggars were everywhere underfoot. Later that week, all communications with her village were cut off. The following day, newscasters pointed out purple blots on an upcountry map, epicenters of the outbreak. Under one was En's village. Within days, the vaccination center arrived, the town was overrun, we began our cereal diet, and prices began their swift ascent. The day En's classes were to begin, the university closed. The quarantine came down. Then the helicopters appeared.

En and I stood on the balcony in the bloodred afternoon, the scene below fit for Dante. The appearance of helicopters set off a contagion of panic. Thousands rushed to the sea, maybe thinking to swim for it. There they thrashed madly, as parasites might in the blood, adding a nautical disaster to the one on land. A rumor spread that sunlight killed the disease. People threw their clothes onto bonfires, smoke hazing upwards to the helicopter blades, naked forms sprinting madly through the streets. Looters smashed storefront windows and guzzled whisky and shoved ice cream down their throats. Copulating couples writhed beneath trampling feet. Stones were hurled at helicopters that hovered too low.

Another announcement. I had an hour. I knew when the helicopters disappeared over the sunrimmed horizon they would not return. The quarantine would not be lifted until the outbreak was over or everyone was dead. Probably it was only a matter of days until the whole country was likewise blockaded. We had to make a run for it.

"Come with me," I said, "They will take us. They have to."

"They will not," she said.

"We will try," I said.

She grabbed the pictures of us. One she slipped down her shirt, next to her heart. The others she ripped up, scattering glossy pieces on the floor.

"The lost spirits. Now they are many," she said. "We must not let them follow us."

"I think they're already on our tail," I said, and pulled her out.

In the hallway a door cracked opened and a man stared at me beneath the security chain. He was a local and had no hope of a helicopter. He handed me a pistol.

"You may need this," he said, and slammed the door before I could thank him. I did not know his name nor could I recognize his face if I saw it again.

The rendezvous was at the university quad, two kilometers away. On the promenade we elbowed our way through the frenzied crowd, slipping on shit and blood and flailing limbs, jostled by whooping peasants leaping the railing to the brown-turned sand to sprint over the low-tide mudflats to the water, me clutching my passport and the pistol. A naked man with a patchwork of spidery purple tattoos running from thighs to cheeks leaped off the railing at me. I brandished the pistol. He snarled and leapt onto the beach. Two fighter jets screamed overhead at very low altitude, banking in the distance. More announcements echoed from the sky but we couldn't hear them in the tumult.

We made it to the street. An on-fire truck careened past to smash into a building. On a stoop a few doors down three small children bawled over a prostrate body, likely their mother, before her skull was split open. I rushed past but En held me back. En squatted by the smallest child, a little boy with no shirt and a bloody mouth. His sister pushed the screaming boy into En's arms. I was certain our chances of escape were doomed, but En would not relinquish the boy nor listen to me. We ran on through the madness. En tripped over a piece of rubble. I held her up with the same grip she used to hold me in the village. I heard her twilling her dialect into the boy's ear. Nearly to the haggard-looking palms fringing campus, we heard popping rifle reports.

At the university gates, soldiers tried to push back the human press. More shots. The crowd retreated, momentarily more fearful of impending instant death in front than a lingering one behind. I pulled En forward through the screaming tripping mass of bodies. We launched ourselves over a few ranks of supine forms and were through to the gates, deep purple scratches bleeding and weltered over in bruises, but still standing. We passed the child through the wrought-iron bars, and the gate cracked enough to allow us through. A squad of soldiers with bayonets fixed closed ranks behind us. We sprinted to the quad as the firing and screaming went on. A helicopter was there and a straggling line of desperate foreigners and hangers-on held out documents to a frazzled captain at a makeshift desk, backed by shifty-eyed soldiers. I dropped the pistol when one lowered his rifle at me.

En held the boy so tightly his wails were muffled and snot ran over her shoulder. We didn't even know his name. But the captain, shouting over the din, wanted to know.

"Ni!" I shouted. "Ni!"

"Your son?" said the captain, pen posed over a sheaf of documents he'd long since stopped filling out.

"Yes," I said. "He's mine."

"And this is your wife?"

"Yes."

He eyed the peasants with down-arched eyebrows.

"Documents, please," he said.

All I had was my passport. I handed it over and said the other documents were lost.

The Captain said, "They are from this country?"

"My son was born here," I said. "I am taking my family home."

"Only foreigners on the helicopter," said the captain.

The volleys and screams just a few hundred meters away grew more intense. The Captain's cheek twitched but he did not look.

"I cannot go without them."

"You will go without them. All foreigners must leave."

"She'll be killed!" I screamed.

The captain gestured to an orderly, who stepped from behind the desk and reached for me with a gloved hand. Eruption of noise from the gates, loud enough to hear over the helicopter, the screeching of twisting metal, another volley of shots. Everyone turned to look, even the captain.

The crowd had burst the gates. It swallowed up the soldiers at the gate and made for the helicopter. The Captain barked orders and the soldiers around us formed a ragged line and raised their weapons. The orderly dropped my arm. We ran for it.

We jumped in as the skids began to leave the ground. Close behind were two teenaged soldiers who'd dropped their weapons. One of them was the orderly. I helped him in as the chopper paused. The crowd engulfed the captain and his small islet of men and came on. The best sprinters made leaping grabs for the skids. The chopper faltered and seesawed. I helped the orderly smash fingers and arms with my heels until they let go and then we were off over the ocean. A few small shapes below were far out, still swimming for it.

We huddled together and no one spoke or looked at each other. We landed somewhere an hour later, the boy asleep on En's lap. The unarmed soldiers were hauled away and we civilians were escorted across a sweltering tarmac to an empty hangar. I feared we would be asked for documents, but instead we were unceremoniously stripped, sprayed with power hoses by rubber-gloved men, and doused in a choking powder that tasted of tar. We were issued garb that looked suspiciously like prison uniforms, then escorted onto boats that took us to a southern island. We lived in medical and diplomatic limbo for half a year, fed by the Red Cross, living in tin huts, drinking rainwater, transforming into a family. But we lived. No documents necessary.

The pandemic passed. A consular officer from the US embassy appeared and offered me a flight home. There was martial law but plenty of work. A few Midwestern cities were contagion-free. My hometown was not one of them. And I was going nowhere without my family. The consular officer told me En and Ni could not possibly accompany me. No one from this country, he said, was going to be allowed into the US for a long time to come.

The coastal town was mostly deserted, but largely still standing. The corpses had been burnt and life was slowly returning, a few shops and a few bicycles. The place had fared far better than the countryside, to which travel was impossible and it was speculated not one in a thousand had survived. My suite had been swept bare by looters and then sullied by the cooking fires of the squatters. Scattered among the cinders and cigarette butts was half a charred bobblehead. And one glossy scrap, last remains of those pictures of us. En clutched it to her breast and pulled Ni back from a pile of glass shards. I swept them aside. We would start here.

CITY OF SCREAMS

ใช้คืน

—1—

The Afghan villagers outside Combat Post Khawji Qasar had never seen an American Indian before. Fascinated by Jackdaw, the old men and children ignored the blacks and whites in his platoon to hover over Jackdaw as he spaded out an irrigation ditch blown up by the Taliban, close enough he could smell their breath, rank with garlic and pukka tea. He called the interpreter over to ask what was going on.

The interpreter said, "They say you look Mongolian. Are you Mongolian?"

"No, man. I'm Lakota."

"You see that city up there?" asked the interpreter, pointing to the ruins that topped the hill on the far side of the combat post, commanding a view of the ragged green valley and the pass clefted between the white peaks ducking and dancing in a serried procession of clouds. "Genghis Khan swarmed over the pass and killed every man and child in that city and gave the women to his soldiers to rape. Then he burned the city. It is called the City of Screams."

"That was like a thousand years ago."

"Your time is not the time of the villagers. To them this happened only yesterday. Genghis Khan was Mongolian. you see."

"And they think I am, too?"

"As I said. You very much look like one."

"Hey, JD," said the sergeant, "this ditch ain't going to dig itself."

"Roger, sergeant," said Jackdaw, leaning back into his shovel. "Well, I didn't have any goddamn thing to do with it. You tell them, all right? Tell them."

The interpreter shook his head sadly. "I am afraid they will not believe me."

Sure enough, when Jackdaw went on patrol, the air grew thick with gesticulation in his direction as the men considered him huddled in doorways leaking smoke from cooking fires. Young boys with toy guns fashioned from scrap metal took aim at him from hard-packed lanes where brackish sewage dribbled into the dust. Women drew their veils and fled, leaving empty buckets at the village well.

Jackdaw got to thinking about the rez back home. Tried to envision those distant days of starvation and defeat, gut-shot old men, violated women, bayoneted babies. Atrocities carried out in the name of the same flag that flapped over Combat Post Khawji Qasar, by the same Army where he was a grunt. No, you couldn't blame those Afghans for their long grudge.

The question was, why didn't he have one?

When a full-bird colonel came on a command inspection, Jackdaw was on guard duty in a tower. He ran his fingers down the rifle pondering a little revenge and was suffused with sudden strange happiness.

"What the hell's wrong with you?" said his fellow in the tower.

"Nothing," said Jackdaw.

"Then wipe that shit-eating grin off your face."

Later, Jackdaw sat in the reeking honey bucket, laptop hot on his thighs, blonde taking it up the ass onscreen. Pictured himself as a Mongolian warrior hoisting that blonde into the saddle, impaling her on his cock at full gallop, yellow hair bunched in his fists, laughing at her screams. He walloped himself so hard his dick chafed and bled.

Soon after, a suicide bomber pulverized Jackdaw's platoon as they humped sacks of cement to a new school building. The heavy sack of cement on Jackdaw's back kept him alive but his legs got splattered with shrapnel. He almost bled out before a medic applied a tourniquet, watching a goat munch on a candy bar wrapper in the rubble as tracers flew overhead and mortars blossomed on the hillsides above the City of Screams.

—2—

Jackdaw slid down the ragged brick wall of White Buffalo Liquor clutching a plastic bottle of vodka, flecks of fresh vomit on his lips, scar-rippled legs throbbing. His shirt was ripped halfway up his arm and crusted with blood from a fall several days old. No one listened to his slurry demands for justice. Just another drunk Indian. When he hit the ground, he blacked out.

Lamar War Bonnet crawled over on hands and knees and pried the bottle from his fingers. He had a long pull, waved to a couple youngsters dropping cases of malt liquor in a pickup to haul back to the reservation. Then Lamar War Bonnet toppled to his side on the cracked asphalt and choked to death on his own vomit.

As Jackdaw woke, the cashier from the White Buffalo stepped around the group gathered around the corpse.

"I told you," said the cashier. "There isn't nothing more I can do. I done called the authorities."

The group let the cashier pass, muttering. Lamar War Bonnet laid there with slack blue lips leaching red bile, trousers stained with shit. Jackdaw pushed aside legs to retrieve his vodka. He sat cross-legged next to Lamar holding the empty bottle until a Highway Patrolman pulled up in a blur of pulsating lights.

"Stand aside, stand aside," the smokey said, curled his lips at the reek of vomit and shit. "Christ on a crutch. Hey. Hey you."

The smokey was talking to Jackdaw. Jackdaw slowly raised his head.

"What?" Jackdaw said.

"Move on. Get away from that body."

Jackdaw looked up at him stupidly. "I'm sitting here."

"Move along, I said."

Jackdaw struggled to his feet, legs pounding with fire, head awash with whirligigs, and stumbled away. It had been nearly a year since Afghanistan, time spent mostly drunk and often as not here in Rattlecreek, home to three liquor stores and one abandoned church, a town which existed for one reason: to peddle poison to his people. The reservation was dry and no whites lived within forty miles of Rattlecreek. Yet here it stood. The liquor stores addled his people into collaborating with their own conquerors, reducing them to drunken serfs in their own homeland.

Time he quit with the goddamned talking.

He staggered to the front of the White Buffalo and ripped off his torn shirt sleeve and stuffed it in the empty vodka bottle. Pulled out his zippo with the 71st Engineers emblem etched on it and lit the rag. He wanted to make a Molotov. He'd seen insurgents do this in Afghanistan.

"Hey!" yelled the smokey, and trotted over. "You there. Stop that!"

The smokey knocked the bottle out of Jackdaw's hand with a nightstick. It shattered on the asphalt and Jackdaw staggered and fell. Yelling onlookers closed in. Fracas ensued, pepper spray misted the air, the smokey shouted into his shoulder mic for backup.

By the time the lawmen pulled out of town, seven residents of the Roubidoux Reservation were on their way to lock-up and three lawmen require stitches. A coroner's van hauled Lamar away. Jackdaw crawled out of a ditch and into Lamar's yellow 1985 Datsun pickup. He raked up the keys from the floor mat and drove back to the reservation.

—§—

Lamar War Bonnet was conveyed in the back of a pickup to the Catholic church house in a hand-built plywood and pine casket.

The casket was too large to fit in the church's narrow entrance. Someone suggested turning the casket rightways up but then it was too tall. So the mourners left the casket upright, facing inside, so Lamar could be listen in and be sprinkled with holy water by the priest.

During the service several flasks made the rounds and the pallbearers dropped Lamar three times getting him back to the pickup. As the procession snaked out of the churchyard, beer cans glinted in every cab.

Jackdaw didn't go. He was partially sober and he hadn't talked in a week. He stood in the deserted churchyard, looking at Lamar's yellow Datsun still parked there.

Alma War Bonnet, Lamar's niece, came out of the church house when the last of the dust from the procession blew away.

"Hi, JD," she said.

"Hi," said Jackdaw. "Listen. I'm through with it."

"With what?"

"With this," he said, and stomped his empty beer can, nearly lurching over with the effort. "Watch."

He stuck fingers down his throat and vomited a thin bile of beer and vodka and peanut butter. Wiped his mouth and felt a little less drunk.

"That's it," he said. "I'm done with that shit forever."

"Come on," said Alma.

She took him by the hand to the Datsun. Drove to a copse of trees down by a creek where they fucked, axles screeching, as dry clods of dirt lumped onto Lamar War Bonnet's casket in the bone orchard.

—§—

Slow and gimpy on his bum legs, Jackdaw hiked back into the hills where the wildflowers exploded in breeze-shaken patches, passing under shelves of limestone with banks of pine clinging ragged to their sides, tangled root skeins cracking the rock.

He stayed in the hills a month, living on spring water and the canned beans and spam Alma humped back to him, until he was sure he lived with no lust for the bottle he'd succumb to. Started doing pushups again and soon got back to three hundred a day. Alma did two hundred.

They ran side-by-side down the dirt roads of the rez, as far as Jackdaw's twitchy legs held out, drawing guffaws and catcalls from government-issue trailers where the stacks of empty bottles reached the window eaves. Feeling good for the first time since he got blown up, Jackdaw fucked Alma with abandon. After, he twirled her blonde hair in his fingers.

Alma had dyed her hair when she was out in Illinois, playing basketball at a community college. She lasted a semester and a half, until she tore her ACL and dropped all her classes. The black roots were slowly edging out the blonde ends. Jackdaw cussed these roots kindly.

—§—

They were in the room Alma shared with her stepsister in her stepmother's trailer. Her step-sister was six. The wall by her bed was covered in Disney princesses printed out from the Internet at school.

Jackdaw said, "I mean it." He ripped Belle down.

"I know," said Alma.

"I don't give a fuck. Do you?"

"No."

Jackdaw's come still squishing inside her, Alma felt a twinge of what women in the City of Screams knew, ravished by fur-clad warriors still spattered with the blood of their fathers and brothers. In the next room Alma's stepmother guffawed to the canned TV laughter.

"Then you're with me," said Jackdaw.

"Yes," said Alma.

"They're going to sing songs about us. I learned one thing from them Afghans. If we don't pull this off, someone after us else will."

—3—

Jackdaw climbs out of Lamar's Datsun. The bed rattles with packing crates full of beer-bottle Molotov's. Alma totes a 9mm pistol and an MP-5 submachine gun. Jackdaw is strapped with two 9mms and an M4. He cashed out a VA disability payment and the last of his combat pay to get a hold of the weapons, buying them in the back room of a flea market from an arms dealer more used to dealing with neo-militias than a nervous, hobbled Indian.

"We're about to tear this motherfucker up," says Jackdaw, "and you want me to get all painted."

"Shut up," says Alma. "You're doing it."

She leads him through the sagging doorway of a jackshack at the tail end of a weed-blown two-tracker. Jackdaw steps over raccoon and deer scat and looks around. Two empty rooms, slats showing through jagged cracks in the wall, pebbles of plaster scattered on the warped floorboards. Jackdaw eases himself to a squat and picks up a pebble, thumbs powder from the edges.

"No one's here," he says. He'd expected some wrinkled elder.

"You noticed," says Alma.

"Who's going to do it, then?"

"Me."

"You? What do you know about painting?"

"Only those assholes who go fancy dancing know how. So I got out a book."

"From the library?"

"Yep. Directions and pictures and everything. Look."

Alma pulls out a thick volume from her backpack, revealing a slice of brown back. She props the book against a wall and sets canisters of grease paint alongside it. Opens to a chapter entitled "The Art of Lakota War." Helpful pages have been dog-eared and attacked with magic marker.

"I'll do you, you do me," says Alma.

—§—

Jackdaw hurls three Molotov's at the glass façade of High Plains Spirits as Alma shoulders open the door to Ace Liquor. Then he shambles into the White Buffalo carrying a crate of four Molotov's. Drops the crate, fires the M4 into the ceiling twice, then slings the rifle over his shoulder.

"Get the fuck out of here!" he shouts to customers staring from the aisles and the clerk gaping from behind bulletproof glass, the clerk who watched Lamar die.

Everyone scrambles for the exit but a quaking fat woman. Plastic whisky bottles tumble from the shelves and skitter across the peeling linoleum floor. Jackdaw grabs the woman's meaty arm and yanks her towards the exit. Grabs a Molotov and lights it.

"Jackdaw?" the woman says. "Jackdaw Le Fourche, what are you doing?"

"Get the fuck out," Jackdaw says.

Jackdaw throws the Molotov. Then another and another and another. He trips on the bottles in the aisle and catches his balance on a shelf. Warm forties of beer shatter on the floor.

Tendrils of blue flame curl into the cheap particleboard as smoke wallows into the rafters. Jackdaw ducks outside coughing. Alma is at the Datsun, grabbing more Molotov's. The clerk stands in the road, watching flames lick his car's windshield. Jackdaw unslings the M4. Switches the safety, shoulders the rifle.

"Hey, what the hell?" the clerk says. "Hey!"

A three-shot burst and the clerk is road kill.

—§—

Smoke from Rattlecreek smears the sky as Jackdaw sits on the vestibule of the shuttered Episcopalian church, rifle across his lap, waiting. Ashes whorl around the banisters of the vestibule. Alma puts her head on his shoulder. A line of people begin to creep back into town, taking pictures with their phones, as the liquor stores collapse in on themselves. Jackdaw is hoping for a lady cop. A blonde one. He looks at Alma.

"You didn't really believe we could get away, did you?" he says.

"No," says Alma. "Not from the start."

"Me neither. I tell you this much. They ain't taking me out of here alive."

"Me either."

Finally they hear a keening siren. Over the far ridge comes a fire truck. Alma hops off Jackdaw's lap. The onlookers flee, taking video as they go.

A Volunteer Fire Department truck howls past the church, screeching to a halt in front of the clerk's body. The volunteer firemen, ranchers and railroaders in real life, jump to the street. Not one is a blonde or a woman.

Jackdaw and Alma squeeze off their whole magazines as the radio shrieks with requests for backup. Just beyond the horizon where the smoke vanishes a long string of sirens are helling for Rattlecreek.

THE LAST LADDER

เกษียณ

Fourth day on the job sprucing up the grounds of a mint-green house on E Street, Roy was touching up the soffit paint when Jeff climbed out of his big Ford diesel pickup and strode to the ladder.

"You all right up there?" Jeff asked.

"I'm all right," said Roy. While Roy had been busy clearing weeds from the rock bed up front, trying not to pull up the petunias with the sandburs and ragweed, Jeff had been showing up and entering the house without knocking where Janice and her daughter Madison lived. Jeff never stayed more than an hour or two, time teenaged Madison spent outside yapping on her phone wearing multicolored bras and smelling of baby powder and lilacs. She never even noticed Roy but Roy's blood lit with desire for the first time in years.

"Come on down, would you?" Jeff said. "Like to talk with you a sec."

Roy hooked the paint can on the ladder and creaked down the steps, pain seething in his back. Needed surgery. Wife dead. Kids run off. Broke. Which explained what he was doing up a ladder at two years shy of seventy. He could remember when this hillside had been a potato field and he a young man sacking spuds fourteen, sixteen hours a day, no sweat.

Jeff watched him with dead oyster eyes. "Guy don't climb a

ladder unless he's got no choice. How many more ladders you think you got in you, old man?"

Roy had actually been thinking about this very thing. Trying to formulate a number. Trying to decide if such a number would get him through winter or not.

"Many as there's got to be, I guess," said Roy.

"What if I was to offer you something a little easier?" Jeff asked.

"I suppose I'd listen."

"I need deliveries run. I give you a bag. You drop it off, bring me a bag back. How's that grab you?"

"What's in the bag?"

Jeff grabbed an earlobe, worked it between his fingers. "Does it matter?"

"Is it drugs?"

Jeff turned. "Forget it."

Roy looked at the paint can swinging on the ladder. However many ladders there were, it'd be too many. "Hold on, now," he said.

—§—

A codger bagman was Jeff's best idea in years. He couldn't believe he hadn't thought of it before. Who looks twice at an old man?

Jeff sent Roy all over Gulpwine, from the old bay-and-gable houses up on the hill to the trailer parks down below. And he gave Roy deliveries out in the country, too, lonely ranch houses twenty miles off the highway and jackshacks jerry-rigged out of campers and plywood. One time he sent Roy to a rest stop, another time the mailbox room of a tiny post office in a two-building town. Folks were surprised to see an old man. Most were nice and held the door for him, the codger said. Once someone gave him a thermos of hot chocolate. Jeff laughed, asked if they threw in marshmallows too.

Jeff paid Roy in soiled twenties, transported to the house in the unregistered Audi Janice drove in for him that week. Jeff had set up Janice and Madison, that slut daughter of hers, in this house to funnel the cash and cars through. Plus blowjobs and the occasional meal and a place to stash the crank. Jeff told Janice she could drive the cars but if she ever touched the crank he'd fuck her ass and kick it out into the alley at the same time. He was looking at Madison when he said this, though. Hers was the ass he really wanted to fuck. Another year or two, he'd try it on. Her bone-idle momma would put up with damn near anything if it kept her from working.

—§—

Roy was home watching college football when the phone rang.

"Got a delivery," Jeff said.

"Tonight yet?"

"Yeah. Take off your cardigan and get up here."

The blacktop was wild with wind that night, gusts rattling the car. By the time Roy got back to the mint-green house it was near midnight and he ached from the effort to keep the car between the white lines. He swallowed a moan as he climbed out of his car, back twitching.

Then an Audi skidded into the driveway, engine a sloppy roar in the quiet neighborhood. Madison staggered out of the driver's seat to the passenger side. When she opened the door, a body tumbled out. Austin, Madison's boyfriend. His head mashed in.

"Help me!" Madison said to Roy. The top two buttons Madison's shirt were loose, exposing a pink bra strap. "Please," she said.

Roy bent over to grab Austin but pain seared his back and he had to straighten up. The front door of the house slapped open.

"The fuck?" Jeff said.

Janice came out on the stoop and screamed and then Madison screamed, too.

Jeff leapt off the stoop and flopped the body back in the car, slamming the car door. Then he shoved everyone inside the house. Roy stood in the front hall trying to keep a grimace off his face, back spasming while Janice and Madison cried together on the couch. Roy could smell the booze on Madison from the hallway.

"What in the actual fuck is going on?" Jeff shouted.

"Beer pongs," said the girl.

"Make sense, goddammit."

"We were doing beer pongs. Out at the lake. Austin couldn't even walk. I started driving us home and he said he was getting sick and I said don't you puke in Jeff's car, he'll fucking kill you." She sobbed, pulled her knees up to her chest.

"Quit your blubbering," said Jeff. "Then what?"

"He stuck his head out the window, and, I don't know. A mailbox or something."

"Is he dead?" asked Janice.

"Yeah, he's fucking dead. And you," Jeff said to Madison, "you dumb cunt, you brought him here."

"I thought you'd know what to do," said Madison, and buried her head in her momma's chest.

"Oh, honey, honey, it's okay," said Janice.

"No, Janice," said Jeff. "It is most definitely not fucking okay. She brought this shit to my house. You don't think the cops aren't going to get interested?"

"You can hide all the crank, Jeff," said Janice.

"Jesus fucking Christ. 'Hide all the crank, Jeff.' Yeah, that's what I bought this house for. So I could hide the crank from it." He raised a hand, then slowly dropped it. "Tell you what. I ain't going back to the joint because of your cunt daughter. And I don't think she'd much like it there, either."

"What are we going to do?" asked Janice.

Jeff looked at Roy. Roy jumped. He'd almost forgotten he was here.

"We got us a hot mess here," said Jeff. "Going to need your help."

Roy felt it all spiraling inside him. Here was a chance to climb his last ladder, ever. "But this isn't no ordinary run."

Jeff crossed the living room in three paces and stood less than a foot off Roy. "What exactly are you saying to me?"

"You got to make it worth my while," he said.

Jeff's smile was a gash in his face. "That right?"

Roy nodded. "Yeah," he said. "That's right."

—§—

Janice and Jeff watched Roy pull out of the driveway in the Audi.

"Are you sure you this will work?" she asked. "How do you know he won't ..."

"Janice," said Jeff, shoving a .45 ACP in a duffel bag. "Shut. The fuck. Up. This is hard time upstate I am saving your bitch daughter from. You remember that."

He wasn't looking at Janice when he said this. He was looking at Madison, prone on the couch, teddy bear blanket wrapped around her. Sure as shit she owed Jeff that ass now.

—§—

Roy drove along watching the white lines waver in the high beams. Mumbling snatches of an old Buck Owens song, ain't it amazing how I love you. Trying to keep the clamp down on his jittery mind, he took the turnoff just short of the Wyoming-Nebraska border past a set of sharp seep draws that gaped black in the moonlight. Austin slumped against the door, smear of gloppy blood down the window.

Headlights blossomed in the rearview. On this long stretch of highway they came on some minutes before Roy could tell it was Jeff's jacked-up Ford.

Jeff had had thirty miles of dark highway to think about Roy having this whole goddamn affair to hold over him. Toddling around town, running his senile old yap. He fingered the .45 in the duffel. No, it could be cleaner than that. That Audi wasn't registered. They couldn't trace it back to him or anyone. Wouldn't the pigs have a good time, trying to figure out how the old man ended in the car with that kid. Probably think he was just some old pervert.

"I told you I know the way," Roy said. "I was driving this road before it was a road."

The big diesel pulled to within feet of the Audi's rear bumper, flooding the car with light, blinding Roy. They came up over a rise and Roy eased off the gas so Jeff could get around him but the big Ford stayed stubborn behind him.

"What in the sam hill?" said Roy. "You want me to lead the way, you don't got to go crowding me."

He accelerated back to cruising speed. Topped Clemmons Ridge where the wind hollered the hardest and the seep draws were black rips in the earth.

That's when Jeff saw his chance. He roared the big roared alongside the Audi, shearing off the side view mirror. Jerked hard on the steering wheel, careening into the smaller car.

"Why, you son of a bitch," said Roy.

The Audi kissed a guard rail and sheared back onto the highway in a shower of sparks. As the diesel came in again Roy slapped the brakes and the big diesel skittered into his lane, taking the Audi's front bumper.

"Come on, you bastard!" Roy shouted. "Come on!"

Roy stomped the accelerator and slammed into the Ford's rear end. The Ford skated into a tailspin in a scud of white smoke, then flipped on its side. Rolled over twice to the curve where it plunged into the ravine.

Roy screeched to a halt. Flipped a U and edged to the asphalt's edge. Wrenched himself out of the Audi. Looked down on the Ford's taillights a hundred feet below.

"Told you I know this road," he shouted. "Bet you didn't see that curve coming." He started into the car, then turned back to the ravine. "Hey, where's my money? Huh? Where?"

No, no money. Only ladders looming out into all the distance ahead.

Unless – those girls. If he brought this car back all nice and clean, like nothing ever happened, they'd pay up. Maybe not even in money. He could see Madison's bra strap edging off her shoulder, smell the lilacs on her.

He popped the passenger door and Austin pitched out. Roy

ponderously bent over, hooked hands in Austin's armpits, and dragged him over to the twisted and broken wire railing. Keeled Austin into the ravine like a sack of spuds and then stood, back atwitter with the shakes.

Convulsions shivering his frame, Roy inched back into the Audi. Reached to close the door and a soft tug of cartilage gave way in his spine and he toppled half out of the car. He knew he wasn't getting up again on his own. He lay on the asphalt in the faint gleam of the Audi's dome light, wind prickly with the taste of oncoming snow.

A GOOD GIRL

ใจจริง

Masaru made it to Miwa's apartment. Stumbled in the door, left arm straight and stiff. Got Miwa out from under the kotatsu. Got her good and woke up. He couldn't believe that cop shot him. He'd never even seen a cop pull a gun before.

Well, goddammit, what'd he been carrying that pistol all this time for, if not to use it? He'd only fired it off a few times, the last being at the O-bon Festival they had out in the sticks a few years back, pretty drunk, missing the trees in the forest. Everyone laughed, called him "Old Blindy." It was true that he was getting pretty old to be as low in the ranks as he was. He hardly needed reminding. He felt like taking a potshot at one of those insolent young punks, like Arawaki, who thought it was so hilarious. But he grimly took it, knowing his temper had kept him from advancing in the first place. And now it didn't matter. Today he'd snapped. Unthinkable, what he'd done.

No help would be coming. No one would aid a cop-killer. Even if the cop hadn't actually died. Just taking a shot at one was so far beyond the pale you couldn't even begin imagining at it. How many times did he get told his temper would ruin him one day? No point pondering. He'd made it here, unhindered and unfollowed. That was something.

"A little higher," he growled at Miwa, who was wrapping a towel around his arm.

"Sorry," said Miwa.

She slid the towel under his armpit and tied it tight. Blood soaked into the purple lettering, which advertised the name of an onsen resort in Kyushu. They'd stayed there together last year, the first time he slept with her. Also, it marked the first time he'd slept with anyone for free.

Although he'd already spent a stupid amount of money on her in actuality. Courting a hostess was an expensive prospect. They expected things – gifts, posh dinners, pocket money. Even one as fresh off the farm as Miwa had been when he met her. He, in fact, had personally approved her hiring. He was pretty tight with the mama-san at the place he'd made his official hostess bar, after it became clear he wasn't going to do much boozing with higher-ups, bullying weak junior members into accompanying him a few nights a week. She was 19 then, so shy and awkward you felt sorry for her. Cute, but hardly beautiful, face round, front teeth crooked, hair stringy no matter how much expensive conditioner her bought her.

He made sure no groping hands molested her while she got her water-trade sea legs, and patiently held cigarettes in his lips waiting for her get the lighter going. Eventually he brought her roses. He felt ridiculous, walking in with the bouquet in his hands and all eyes on him. Subordinates laughed and didn't try to hide it. Miwa saw him coming and didn't look up or thank him. He shoved them at her and stomped out. He didn't come back for two weeks.

He didn't believe a young girl could want him, a grizzled 42, always looking like he hadn't slept in days, jutting chin, cherry blossom and demon tattoos running up to the edge of every collar and cuff and hem-line, eyes even hookers labeled cruel. He tried for her anyway. She didn't quit or run away as everyone, including the mama-san, predicted. Eventually, she consented to appear outside the bar with him and then the cash really started dropping. Some time later, they went to that resort. The place was stupidly expensive – he finished off the remainder of his savings. Though, it was nice having the baths all to himself, spineless worker bees beating hasty exits after one glance at his tats. One ran out with foamy shampoo running down his neck.

The sole souvenir of that weekend was now around his arm going maroon.

Masaru was expecting a barrage of questions from the girl. But Miwa didn't say anything, nor look especially surprised. He had shown her the pistol a few times. He liked watching her face as she stroked it. It was a nice change of pace. He definitely couldn't flash it around when he was working. Being considered too old for much street work, he slunk humbly around the offices, shouting "Yes, sir!" to every little whim a higher-up had, fetching cigarette packs and pouring cups of tea and fielding phone calls.

He didn't like to think of all the punks he deep-bowed to now, ones who used to bow to him. Arawaki especially. People thought there must be something wrong with him, since no one promoted him; no one promoted him because they thought something was wrong with him. He tried to not to think about it. Wasn't room for everyone at the top.

But it kept on building up and up in him. All the more so because he didn't resort to the usual outlets. Didn't beat Miwa, for instance. He might have smacked her once or twice, but he didn't make a practice of it. The girl, knowing what he was, seemed to expect it. He drank, but his face always went all red and after a few, he got all the hangover and none of the drunk. He got in his fair share of fistfights, but only won about half the time.

Miwa made green tea. He sipped at it, staring at the muted TV screen. He tried to move his arm. It was too stiff to go and pain ran up his shoulder and bounced down his spine. He considered the syndicate doctor in Hyakunin-cho. But that old man normally did nothing more than treat ankles sprained drunk or fingers dislocated encouraging a deadbeat to pay up. Hard to say if he could handle a gunshot wound. An aboveground clinic was out of the question. Masaru was pretty sure they were legally required to report gunshot wounds. Besides, he'd been down in the underworld so long, he no longer existed above. A clinic would ask for a national insurance card or some other form of legitimate ID. He couldn't remember when he'd last had one of those.

"Does it hurt?" Miwa asked, folding her legs beneath her, kneeling next to him on the floor.

"Sure it does," Masaru said. "I got shot."

"Did you shoot anyone?"

"That's a hell of a question," he said.

"I just wanted to know. Since you've ... since I've seen it so many times."

He grunted. His arm pulsated madly.

"Can I see it now?" she asked.

"No," he said.

"What are you going to do?"

"I'm going to drink this tea."

He did, then set the cup on the kotatsu. With his good hand he got out his phone. He flipped it open. Nothing. Arawaki had been there. Seen the whole thing. Then ran the opposite direction. No doubt he was still running, only now it was his goddamn yap. The whole syndicate would know about it by now. No question about it – he was cast out. They'd be cursing him for the shame and trouble he was bringing on them. This was just the sort of public nuisance the syndicate tried to avoid. One dead cop. Guess that counted. Well, okay, one winged cop. Who was plenty alive when he ran out the door. You didn't die from getting shot in the leg. A Chink would have been better. Goddamn Chinks. Strutting around like they owned a piece of the place, slitting throats and pushing that junkie shit. No one would have kicked up much fuss over a shot-up Chink.

"Some whisky," he said to Miwa.

Miwa got up and went into the kitchen area, bringing back a bottle, glasses, a tray of ice.

"No ice," he said.

She poured out a generous slug and Masaru tossed it back. He felt the usual wobbly sickness and his face got hot. A distraction, at least. Miwa watched.

"Have some," Masaru said, pouring out another measure.

"Okay," she said, and drank it down.

They sat there and the TV was silent and outside tires squealed and Masaru jumped. Then it was quiet. He wondered if he could amputate his own arm. No, guess not. You'd need a hacksaw, wouldn't you?

"Another one," he said.

Miwa poured it out.

Probably his demon-head tat, centerpiece on his shoulder, was fucked up. He should get his jacket and shirt off, see. He polished off the whisky and was instantly lightheaded and regretful. He stood up and it got a whole lot worse, the room sloping and spiraling. He tried to steady himself. Miwa gave him an arm. He leaned on her. Her eyes were strong and sturdy. She was a good girl.

"Help me get this off," he said, unzipping his jacket.

His arm felt like it might explode in a splash of blood and bone as she loosened the towel. His good arm slipped out of the jacket sleeve, but when Miwa began pulling on the other sleeve, pain shot up though him like a steadily bursting ball of flame. He clenched his teeth and just managed not to fall over. When she pulled his shirt off his arm, he thought he might black out. He leaned against the wall, lightning-bright explosions on the back of his eyelids. Finally he looked at the wound. Sticky blood was caked everywhere. The hole was at the demon's left eye. It was smaller than he imagined. He bet the cop had a bigger one. 9mm will put a good-sized hole in you.

His 9mm. Special delivered from Italy. Sometimes, getting sick-mean after he'd had a few, he put it up on the bar in the hostess club. Left it there for an hour, two, let liver-necked salarymen pretend to not ogle it out of the corner of their beady little eyes. Once he let the mama-san hold it, but that damn woman drank too much. She almost dropped it. Now anyone who looked like they might think about pretending to touch it ran the risk of swallowing their teeth. Well, that was before.

"Get that towel back on there," he said, voice tinny in his own distance.

She wrapped it around his arm. As she finished, Masaru wondered if you could etch in a new tat over scar tissue.

Although it wouldn't matter if his arm was going to get cut off. Goddammit, that was stupider thinking than he needed. He sat down, had some more tea, tried to keep the cup steady in his fingers. Then he heard the sirens.

They were whining off in a distance you had to concentrate at. Maybe he could still make a run for it. He looked doubtfully at Miwa clearing off the tea things, not yet noticing. She'd have to drive. Couldn't trust himself at the wheel now. Did the girl even know how to drive? He had no idea. He'd have to find out now. If he was going to go.

"Leave that," he said, pointing at the tea pot.

She set it down beside him.

He got himself up, went over to the window, pulled the curtains shut. Be better if this wasn't the first floor. Though it made the rent, which he paid, a lot cheaper. The sirens, plenty of them, got louder. Miwa came out of the kitchen area. They looked at each other across the room. By the time he got out from behind a prison wall, he'd be old. Already he was abandoned and it would be infinitely worse years down the road, a crippled-up ex-gangster with no gang. With nothing.

"They're coming for you, aren't they," Miwa said. It wasn't a question.

"Yeah," said Masaru. "Go on. Get out of here. Or they'll take you with me."

Miwa shook her head.

"Go," said Masaru. "I'm too much trouble to you. You're young. Get out of here."

"I'm staying with you," said Miwa.

He eyed her coldly and found no insincerity.

"Then it's you and me," said Masaru.

They sat down at kotatsu. He fingered the glass of whisky but didn't drink any. She touched his shoulder and he didn't shrug her off. The sirens were outside.

"Take a look," he said.

Miwa went over to the window, cracked the curtain.

"A whole lot of police," she said. "An ambulance."

The apartment faced the street. The sliding door out to the

verandah looked out on a little patch of grass and some shrubs. It wasn't going to be hard to get in here. The question was whether they'd come in shooting. Masaru had no idea how the police went about these things. They had their world, he had his. Harsh voices outside. A sharp rap at the door. He thought he was ready for it, but he jumped.

"Okada Masaru," came a Megaphone Voice. "Do we have the honor of addressing Okada Masaru?"

"You're goddamn right you do," yelled Masaru.

Miwa grabbed his good arm.

"This is the Metropolitan Police. Please be so good as to open this door."

"Not on your fucking life. Back the fuck away from the door or I'll shoot it up."

Shuffling of feet and weighty presences outside.

"I repeat. Your presence is kindly requested outside," said Megaphone Voice.

"Back off! I mean it! Back the fuck off or I'll start shooting! "

He knocked over a lamp with a flailing arm. The bulb shattered as it hit the floor. Miwa watched him wide-eyed.

"Goddamn cops," Masaru mumbled, half to himself, half to her. "Trying to order me around. That's how this whole goddamn thing got goddamn started."

The two of them listened. Plenty of cops seemed to be mingling outside. The sirens stopped but there were rhythmic red flashes on the curtains. It was still dark, a good half-hour until dawn. Masaru squatted down in the corner furthest from the door.

"What now?" asked Miwa, squatting beside him, looking at him with something it took him a moment to place, it'd been so long since he'd seen it – respect, possibly admiration.

"We shut up for a minute, first off," he said, voice gruffer than he meant it to be.

"We once more respectfully request the honor of your presence," said Megaphone Voice. "You are to ..."

Megaphone Voice went on for a while and then went silent. The first slivers of light began to outline the curtain. They could hear helicopters overhead. A spotlight flashed down for a few seconds, lighting up the window bright enough to blind, then disappeared. They were on the first floor of a ten-story apartment block. Not much to see. After, there were no more spotlights, but they could hear helicopters far off and above. Probably the press.

Well, this was the sort of thing that made the news. Him in the news – there was something he'd like to see. It was going to incur the massive displeasure of pretty much all his associates, but it was too late to do anything about that now. Besides, there were some things they didn't know about him. Like how he wasn't going to eat shit the rest of his goddamn life. Did they think he would? He hadn't planned on making his stand like this, but the moment had come and he'd goddamn well taken it. The TV cast an iridescent patch of blue. The third of the screen he could see exerted an irresistible gravity on his eyeballs.

"Turn that off," he said to Miwa.

She crawled over on all fours to the kotatsu, grabbed the remote, and flicked the screen black. Masaru noticed a faint trace of the perfume he'd gotten her for her birthday. She came back and reached over his head to flip on the kitchen light. A sickly yellow rectangle glowed over their heads. Masaru had his hands in his lap, sitting with legs folded beneath him. He couldn't get comfortable sitting any other way. Miwa leaned against him and stroked his arm.

After a while, Megaphone Voice came back.

"This is the Metropolitan Police. You are to exit slowly, with hands raised. You must comply immediately. Repeat. You must comply immediately."

A cold cold throb was edging slowly up his arm. He could no longer will his fingers to move.

"Whisky," said Masaru.

Miwa went for it. Coming back on her hands and knees, her hair hung around her face and in the weak light, he thought her quite pretty.

"If Fukuda Miwa is inside, she is ordered outside

immediately," said Megaphone Voice. "Fukuda Miwa, you are in grave danger. Repeat ..."

They said nothing. Masaru sipped at his whisky. The dry fire of it seared the roof of his mouth and the walls of his throat. He retched, swallowed vomit back. Miwa patted his back. So this was the night he couldn't choke down any more whisky. Some night for it. He was suddenly terribly thirsty.

"Water," he said. "Get me some water."

Miwa crawled into the kitchen area.

"Fukuda Miwa. We believe you to be present inside. We assume you are being held against your will. Remain calm. Okada Masaru, you are hereby ordered to release her immediately. It is shameful to punish the innocent for your folly. Cease and desist."

"Innocent, are you?" he said to Miwa, back by his side now, sipping at the water.

She beamed a smile all out of proportion to the situation. He wished he'd been kinder to this girl. Or had more time to be kind to her in.

"If they force their way in," he said, "keep your head down."

She said, "What will you do?"

"You just keep your head down. Get into the kitchen. After, tell them I held you by force."

"But you didn't."

"I know, goddammit. But they'll go easier on you if they think I did."

"I want to go with you."

"Fukuda Miwa," said Megaphone Voice. "Remain calm ..."

"You can't go where I'm going," said Masaru.

"Oh," said Miwa. "I think I can."

A white wave of tripping darkness washed over him and he had to lean against her. He wasn't going to be able go on making decisions. He'd just have to believe her.

Steadied back out, he said, "I'm not walking out of here. You understand?"

"I'm not stupid," she said.

"Okada Masaru, this will serve as your last warning. You must immediately ..." said Megaphone Voice.

"You're a good girl," Masaru said.

"... last warning ..."

"Don't talk," said Miwa, not looking at him, running a gentle finger down his leg.

Megaphone Voice shut up and all they could hear was the dull thumping of the helicopters. Creeping cold was moving into his neck. He reached into his leather bag with his good arm. He reached past his fingernail clippers – necessary since the oyabun had snapped a subordinate's finger ninety degrees for having dirty fingernails in his presence – to his straight-edge razor. He was sometimes out all night on the syndicate's business. He couldn't be unshaven. Nor he could he be carrying around some safety razor a woman could shave her arms with.

And he still had his knife. Straight off the movies and ordered direct from Utah, America. He slid it out of the sheath. The hilt was whittled down to a perfect fit for his hand.

"You know how we're going to do this?" he said to Miwa.

"Yes," she said.

"Just pull it across hard," he asked.

"I will," she said.

"You take the razor. It'll be easier for you. I just sharpened it."

"Yes," she said.

"Wait for me to nod. Don't think. Keep your mind clear. Just do it."

"Not a thought," she said. "Not a word."

Maybe it was better this way, with no gun. He'd shocked the shit out of himself, firing it. So much so that he'd thrown it deep down an alley as he rushed out of the building, away from the cop wriggling on the floor. The worst thing he could have done. Impossible to think of facing any associates – any of them – now. He'd broken the unwritten rules, shooting a cop. Unforgivable, but understandable. Who didn't sometimes think about wasting one of those officious bastards? But there were other rules, written in his guts. Break them, and he was worse than worthless. He was an enemy to himself, which made him an enemy to the syndicate that made him what he was. Without the syndicate, he was nothing. Less than nothing.

Outside it was the quiet of dawn. The distant thump of the helicopters was gone and there were no lights flashing on the curtains.

"It won't be long now," he said.

"No," she said.

"Haven't you got anything else to wear?" he asked.

She was wearing blue jeans and a light camisole, accenting the heavy curve of her breasts.

"It's a little late for a kimono, Masu-chan," she said, smiling, revealing the pointy incisors generally considered to be her main charm point.

"Put on a sweater, at least. Cover up. You don't want to look like a slut."

She crawled over to the closet, slid open the door. She reached into the darkness, extracting a light black sweater. She came back, folded her legs below her. They sat with knees touching. She put the sweater on and picked up the razor from the floor.

"How's that?" she said.

"It'll do," he said.

Outside the door were massed feet, trying to be quieter than they could manage. Something shrieked through the window in a shower of broken glass. The room flooded with acrid white smoke and the first bright beams of dawn crashing over the rooftops. Masaru was nearly blinded in the white-light of it. He hurled the teapot in the general direction of the door. The charging outside paused at its shattering crash.

Masaru grabbed the knife and said, "Hold your goddamn breath!"

His throat contracted saying it. He couldn't stop the choking that gurgled up his throat. His eyes brimmed over with tears and Miwa went blurry in his vision. He felt for her chin and got the blade up against her throat. Miwa's fingers were on his cheek and on his neck was a thin metallic coolness. He leaned in, nodded his chin against Miwa's tensed knuckles. His shoulder bumped against the door jamb. The reverberating pain made the stroke of his hand like that of three men.

HARD ENOUGH

ไม่มีธรรมะ

(EXCERPTS FROM A BAD LIFE)

—1—

Sidestepping an old bicycle vendor halted on the canal bridge, the tourist entered a narrow soi with a hand held over sunglasses. He tripped over the uneven flagstones, heavy backpack jolting on his shoulders and a big fanny pack jostling his belly. One hand clenched a badly folded map. The sledgehammer sun of tropical two o'clock left the tourist's T-shirt and Khmer scarf sodden with sweat.

Shacks constructed from plywood and tin and packing crates lined the *soi*. A curtain of smoke hung in the soupy air. The tourist skipped over dog shit as plastic bags tangled in his ankles and mangosteen skins smushed under his sandals. Vicious soi curs sprawled in the shade barely perked their heads at his passing.

Folks escaping the boil in their shacks lounged in doorways and on makeshift stoops beneath multicolored tarps emblazoned with campaign ads ("Rangorn, Change for Bangkok!"). Old women spit betel nut juice and recalled their teeth and men sipped at used medicine bottles of rice whisky, bangs flicked by clacking electric fans. No, anymore you couldn't go anywhere in Bangkok without spotting a farang. They were like the mayflies that swarmed after a monsoon rain, a sticky annoyance.

A gaggle of children squatting beside a stream of brackish

sweat shop runoff yelled with mild enthusiasm, *"Farang! Farang!"*

The farang smiled and raised a limp hand and a buzzing scooter nearly clipped him. Heads peered into the hot glare all down the lane but the farang kept to his feet by grabbing a shack pole. Two women sitting cross-legged on a mat in the shade tittered with hands to mouths. The farang straightened, grin creasing his whiskered cheeks, and said something.

"I got no idea what you're saying, pinkbody," the first woman said.

"Ki nok chai mai," said the second. "You're broke, ain't you?"

The farang mimed taking a drink, making glugging sounds with his throat.

"Our pump's broken," said the first.

"Now we have to buy our own water, see," said the second.

"You probably couldn't drink it anyway," said the first. "You'd get sick as a dog."

"Ma ma!" said the second. "The dog comes! Get it?"

Tears squirted from their eyes as they guffawed and the farang stepped back into the soi, smile melted to an uneasy grimace. He held a finger to his nose, bead of sweat jiggling there, considering. He looked across the bridge to the thoroughfare choking in the exhaust of gridlocked buses and scooters and taxis, then shrugged and plunged deeper into the soi.

Map damp in his hand, he was nearly run down by another scooter honking madly as it veered around him. He lofted an apologetic hand to the rider's backside and approached a youngish-looking girl.

A kid doddered at her ankles and another was out where the Buddha only knew, running the sois with a pack of fellow delinquents. The girl had once worked in a noodle shop on a congested avenue and farang tourists used to take pictures of her laboring over the giant pots. She'd never gotten used to the pinkbodies and when this one loomed near she shrank back. Still she could see herself in his sunglasses, distended and leering. It occurred to her that maybe this was how the farang saw her.

The farang jabbed a hairy finger at the map. Some of the locales were marked in Thai but this meant nothing to the girl. She'd never looked at map of Bangkok in her life. She stepped back, which the farang must have taken as an invitation because he stepped forward. Lucky for her, he bashed his forehead on a crossbar. The toddler started to wail. The farang retreated again as the girl hoisted the child to a hip.

He headed back down the lane. The menagerie of faces swiveled with him. Among them a man who set aside his newspaper and did not look away when the farang caught his eye. The tourist went to the man's shack, halted at the border of his shade, whiskers furrowed by his grin again, miming for a drink again. The man got up.

"Sure, you hairy bastard," he said. "I got some. Wait here."

He kicked off his sandals and pushed the thin door hanging aside and went inside. His shack was a standard three-roomer, one front room and two smaller ones propped over the canal in back. One was a latrine with hole in the floor, the other a kitchen with a one-ring burner. He grabbed an unopened bottle and turned to the front room. The farang already stood there.

The man almost yelped because the oaf still wore sandals, scummy with soi filth. Until he saw the Glock with a fat silencer pointed at his guts. He dropped the bottle. The gun burped three times.

The farang straddled the carcass and tattooed two more rounds into its forehead. Even with the silencer the slugs thwacking into plywood were audible all down the soi. He returned the pistol to the fanny pack and grabbed the water bottle that had rolled to his feet. He ripped off the lid and stuck it in his pocket and had a long slug.

The faces had vanished when he stepped back outside. He picked up the map, folded it neatly, inserted it in a cargo pocket of his baggy shorts. The old bicycle vendor down the lane rang his bell, trying to drum up business. A black Benz with opaque windows cruised up behind him. The horn sounded lightly, once. The bicycle vendor squeezed his contraption onto an empty stoop to let the sedan past.

It halted for the farang. The back door popped open and the farang shed his heavy pack and climbed inside and the door swung shut. The Benz purred away. The bicycle vendor slowly pumped down the empty soi.

—2—

We were supposed to be making a message out of this mark, so we tied him up and worked him over good for two days running. We didn't ask him anything. We knew we were just going to shoot him in the head when we were through. He knew it, too.

I could feel the crew watching me because it was only my third job. Well, that and I'm a halfbreed. As far as they knew, I was only back in the mother country looking to feast on easy spoils. I had to prove otherwise.

It got messy in that blood-reeking cement room. I didn't know what I was doing. No one showed me. The crew wanted to see if I was hard enough to figure it out myself. So I did. Then I walked out, sat down at the card table, and took their money. And when it was time, I put a cyanide pill down his throat. Let him start foaming before I shot him in the head. The crew liked that.

Still, after we dumped the body, I booked it out of Bangkok sporting a serious case of the black-ass. I wasn't sure I could handle this life. The boss called. Said to hang low. You'll hear from me when there's more work, he said. Don't leave the country.

I ended up in a little coastal town called Chang Saen. That's where I met Nan.

Nan came from a two-room wooden shack, an alkie father, six year's schooling and a long string of under-the-table jobs. Nature compensated her with good posture, mocha-smooth skin, and a smile that could knock you into next Sunday. One day she walked out of the Nike sweatshop to put those tools to use. She worked go-go bars for three years before she hooked the old bastard Bob.

Nan told me all this while we were sitting out on the pier, drinking beer. She slipped a few sleeping pills in Bob's Viagra bottle and prayed for bingo. If she got lucky and Bob conked out, she'd go over to the local side of town, wondering what she'd done in a past life to deserve this.

"Horseshit," I said. "No one deserves anything."

She had another sip of beer, looked me over. "You're a hard one," she said.

"No I'm not."

"You're not in trouble, are you? On the run from something?"

"Just myself."

"Are you healthy? Your body functions properly?"

"Let's give it a whirl. My bike's right there."

Back in my hotel room, we got down to business. After, we laid on the damp sheets and I said, "Jesus Christ. You're lucky you don't kill that old bastard."

"I'm not lucky," she said.

Nan's slick body remained imprinted on mine long after she left. I sat on the edge of the bed, slowly sipping the dregs of her beer. Thinking about the round of jobs I'd done, the round of jobs to come. All the work I could handle, the boss had told me. The black-ass came rolling back pretty fast.

—§—

I went down to the beachside café where Bob and his cronies passed their pointless days. He had all his hair, thirty extra pounds, and a pretty bad limp. Nan helped him to his table. He talked like he was from Minnesota. Wicked the sweat from his forehead with a crumpled handkerchief like he was, too.

I sipped coffee and watched Nan not looking at me, watched Bob give an apish grin every time he looked at her, sausage stuck in his teeth. She put her head on his shoulder, laughed when he laughed. He handed over his wallet, she performed deft extractions. I got tired of the show and shoved off.

—§—

Nan and I took to meeting up on the local side of town as often as she could swing it. I would sit down at a noodle stall. At first the noodle seller thought I was a confused tourist and tried to direct me to the swank hotels and air-conditioned restaurants. Then Nan came roaring up on a scooter.

"I never get to eat real food," she said, shoveling down rice noodles and spicy pork. "The stuff Bob makes me eat. Cheese and bread and grease. Disgusting."

"Are you coming tonight?"

"Depends on the pills, darling."

"Why don't you come over now and not go back?"

She laughed. "Where were you when I had only one shirt in the rain? He's got money. He's going to marry me. What are you going to do? What do you even do, anyway?"

I had no answers for her.

—§—

Nan came over in a maternity sundress, toting shopping sacks.

"Look!" she said.

She showed me a teeny baby T-shirt, festooned with dancing pink penguins.

"Does the old bastard know?" I asked.

"Yes," she said.

I sat there thinking. I could go straight. No more jobs. I'd figure out how.

"Sit down," I said. "We have plans to make."

Nan gnawed a pinky. "You're forgetting Bob."

"Bob can't think it's his. You can't think it's his."

"Of course not, darling. But what difference does that make?"

"I'll kill him, then. I'll kill him and we'll get out of here. How about that?"

"Oh, darling," she said, "don't act stupid." She straddled my lap, put her breasts in my face. "Better get your fill of these before they turn into udders."

I started to, but then she jumped up.

"Oh!" she said. "I have to pee!"

She scampered to the bathroom. Her purse was sitting on the bed. I rummaged inside. Found that bottle of Viagra.

—§—

Down at the café the old bastard was bragging to his cronies about how he'd made his mark in two countries, boy. Nan sat at the table smiling. Bob rubbed her belly. I paid for my coffee. Hopped on my bike and rode out of Chang Saen.

The old bastard would pop that cyanide pill any day now.

—3—

The two Russian girls were right where Charti said, lounging on beach chairs down by the water across from Starbucks, passing a tall bottle of beer back and forth. I dashed off a text then tossed my cigarette and padded through the sand of Pattaya Beach, at a sideways angle so they could see me coming. When I stopped in front of their chairs the girls sat up. One of them had a cat in a top hat tattooed on her left shoulder. The other had a hooknose.

"If you want to live," I said in Russian, "listen to me."

—§—

My name is Hiram Van. My current passport says elsewise, but that's my name. Just a few minutes earlier I had been getting half-cocked in the Sapphire Shark Go-Go when Charti texted me the two Russian girls had finally shown.

Fah, the slinky go-go girl I'd taken back to my hotel five nights in a row, was onstage romancing the poles to "Back In Black," all sequins and lace and saddle-brown skin. You can't sit in a go-go in Thailand all night not drinking or taking anyone home. As cover went, I've had worse.

Those two girls had popped a mobster a roofie during a three-way back in Mother Russia and filched his cash and laptop. Whatever was on that hard drive had kept them on the run for a couple months now. Still, they weren't the kind to hibernate in hotel rooms, slipping out for plates of rice late at night. Three nights ago Charti spotted them down on the beach, but they were gone by the time I got there. So I set up camp in the Sapphire Shark. I trusted Charti to find them before someone else did.

Charti was a hustler all right, gold King Chulalongkorn medallions strung around his neck, sporting flip-flops and a baggy tank top, and he knew every pimp and pusher along Pattaya Beach. He called me "sir" when he sold me the hot iPhone he'd just texted me on, but he never stood too close, like he expected me to cause a crime scene any minute.

I slid the iPhone back in my pocket and called for the bill and finished watching Fah promising paradise for a few thousand baht. I told the waitress to keep the change and stood up adjusting my fanny pack. Fah smiled at me, long and hard. I nodded to the mamasan on the way out. The mamasan didn't nod back.

Outside I threaded the stalls selling T-shirts and Buddhas and porn to tourists, practicing Russian phrases in my head. I'd been practicing for two weeks. The crew was on holiday for the rainy season but I was raised by workaholic ranchers and I felt uneasy if I wasn't on a job.

Dodging tuk-tuks and pickup taxis and motorbikes across Beach Road I could tell I was a lot more loaded than I ought to be. I stopped to toke a cigarette, ease the whirligigs out of my head. Across the road I could hear the last licks of "Back In Black."

"Hey sexy hansum man" called the hookers and ladyboys tarted up in the shadows. Pimps and thieves squatted on the benches smoking as drunk Arabs and Swedes and Aussies stumbled past to bargain with the whores and pushers. An international flesh bazaar, one you could melt right in to. That's what those two Russian girls were probably thinking. I understood. Halfbreed Thai-American mongrel like me, I operated under the same M.O.

—§—

The tattooed girl said something to hooknose. Then something to me. I didn't understand a word.

"I know who you are," I said. "If you want to live, listen to me."

The two girls were holding hands and looking at me.

"If I can find you," I said, "they will too."

That was the end of my Russian. The two girls exchanged a few phrases. The one with the tattoo said something to me. It sounded like a question. I had no answer.

Hooknose jumped from her chair fast as a bony antelope. Almost knocked me over on account of the whiskeys at the Sapphire Shark. I belted her in the face, got her back in the chair. Pretty sure I broke her jaw but it wasn't going to matter to her long. Up on the promenade a couple ladyboys looked at the chairs and then me and then walked away.

The tattooed girl blubbered. "Please," she said in English. "Please."

"No," I said.

A sleek jet boat gunned into the beach. The tattooed girl threw the beer bottle at me. I caught it in the air. A couple Russians jumped from the prow. One of the Russians pushed past me and pistol-whipped the tattooed girl. The other one scooped up hooknose from the chair. The girls didn't kick and they didn't scream. The fight was gone out of them. The Russians waded into the water and threw the girls onboard then eased the boat back out into the inky water.

I readjusted my fanny pack and walked back up the beach and crossed Beach Road to the tourist stalls. Charti would text me when the money was wired.

THE SCABROUS EXPLOITS
OF CYRUS & GALINA VAN,
HELLBENT WEST DURING THE THIRD
YEAR OF THE HARROWS, 1876

นักล่าสมบัติ

Hard times, ain't it, when a man loses both his six-shooters making corpses of two men and a boy whose voice had yet to drop and comes away with such slim trimmings. A single gold doubloon and a few coins of silver, quickly gone to victuals. But Cyrus travels on without hurry, certain his pursuers are dispirited. These are no times for bands of armed men to find welcome anywhere, whatever justice they ride for.

On such a road Cyrus can scarcely tell who makes for a mark and who only busted and of no interest. Until an innkeep sets out a whisky bottle and takes up the doubloon without balking.

"I can change this out for you square," the innkeep says.

Cyrus unsheathes his knife as the innkeep fiddles with a safe in the back room. Leaps the bar catlike on one hand. The innkeep whirls round swinging a shillelagh inlaid with a crucifix. Cyrus feints and cuts him. Cuts him again. The innkeep flops on the floor. Medallions and goblets and necklaces spill from the safe on a river of coins.

A serving girl stands solemn in a gingham dress at the threshold, broom in hand. Thin as a colt, wiry arms, a crooked nose.

"You are right quick," she says. "I seen plenty of men fall drunk on that bar but never one jump it."

She does not resist when Cyrus grabs her, points the knife at her eyeball.

"Where's the guns?" Cyrus asks.

"Locked up," says the girl.

"Unlock them, then."

She squats by the innkeep and pushes aside his slack head, hems of her skirt dragging in blood, ripping free a key on a silver chain. She unlocks an ornate holster from a chest of drawers at the dead man's bedside.

"He had it made special," she says.

The holster smells of soft soapy kid leather. It houses a six-shooter, sheeny and never used the once. The girl hands Cyrus a bandolier of shells. Cyrus loads the piece with easy skill. Cocks and levels it at the girl's forehead. She shivers but stands her ground.

"You got ideas other than shooting me?" the girl says.

"I got a idea or two," says Cyrus.

He grabs the girl by the hair. Jerks her along out front. Pushes the damask aside, looks down the road. It is deserted. He thrusts the entranceway bolt home and releases the girl. She hawks a gob of phlegm to the dusty floorboards.

"I told that son of a bitch and I told him," she says. "Someone was coming for me. You're the one."

"I ain't no one. Hike them skirts."

Cyrus ruts her on the common table. She keeps her skirts pulled up as he grunts hard in her ear. When they finish, Cyrus marks the blood splotched on the table.

"I took you for a tart," he says.

"I ain't a tart," she says. "He was saving me up. Wanted to collect on the dowry. I ain't even his daughter."

"That so?"

"Yes. I only bided here cause Ma and little Elsa took the galloping fever and I nowhere else to go. You're the one now, sure."

She learned the lesson by rote as on the road with Ma and Elsa, Ma taking on as many men as necessary for their keep. Ma constantly repeated that the first man you lay with, him you hang on to. Whatever the cost. After that first one's gone, it don't much matter.

Cyrus hitches up his trousers, uncorks the whisky, has a long pull. Weighs whether to test out the six-shooter on her gut, and if he ought to rut her again first. She meets his gaze and he likes her some for the gesture. Has another suck of whisky. Then escorts her to the back room. Culls coins from the mess and drops them in the girl's obligingly held-out skirts.

The girl pries open the innkeep's fingers for the doubloon. "Don't you want your coin?"

Cyrus snorts. "Faker than a three legged snake. He ought to of known it."

"I got to go with you," says the girl. "You're the one. I just got to."

"That right?" says Cyrus.

"I'll make you look respectable on the road. Look." She plucks two golden rings from the floor. Wedding bands. "Here," she says. "Respectable."

She takes Cyrus's bespattered left hand and slips the ring on. It fits. Then she rings her own hand. Cyrus looks at the band. It comes to him that the girl is right. Brigands don't tote along wives. Respectable on the road. Respectable when it comes time to reclaim the spread out west.

"What's your name?" he asks.

"Galina. You?"

"Cyrus."

"We got a last name, Cyrus?"

He hesitates. He has thought a good deal on this but has yet to say the name aloud. "Van," he says finally. "The name is Van."

—§—

They ride hard down the road, Cyrus not sparing the pace, coin purse bumping satisfyingly against his mare Drue's withers as he drains the pilfered whisky bottles. Galina keeps up on an unnamed stallion taken from the innkeep's stable. They lope past prairie schooners once westward-bound, now facing east, burnt and shat upon. The pair ruts in copses and dells. One night in the act they are lit into by a pack of feral dogs which

Cyrus beats off with a branch, trousers about his ankles. Not the worst Cyrus has seen on the road and he still sports an erection when he turns back to Galina.

Some days later the pair reaches a settlement at an elbow bend in the road. A shrill wind rips away the last autumn leaves and the branches rasp over rickety shacks. The only light dribbles from a smithy window.

The blacksmith swings open the door agleam with sweat, oversized right arm clutching a hammer. Galina's amber eyes glint in the firelight. From five hundred leering customers back at the inn she knows what her looks promise men and true to the pattern the smith makes her welcome, barely glancing at Cyrus. Cyrus grasps the calculus and strolls to stable the horses alongside the smith's mules. Rain patters on the roof as he stands stroking Drue's nose. Only green broke and Cyrus her first rider. Cyrus unrings his finger and caresses the chafed skin there and thinks about riding on alone. Instead he goes inside.

In the stifling smithy Galina sits near the bellows, chin resting on her knees, calves exposed beneath her skirts, watching the smith shape a plow blade. The smith keeps looking at her and misses the mark several times.

After a while he tamps down the bellows and pulls on a workman's frock. Takes ham and hard rye from a shelf which he cuts in thick slices and hands to Galina and Cyrus. A silvery grit dusts everything. Obeying long habits of service, Galina fetches a bowl of water. The water tastes metallic as does the food. The fire in the bellows dies down to coals and casts a light of long shadows.

"Come a far piece?" the smith asks.

"Aye," says Cyrus.

"Where you headed, you don't mind me asking?"

"West."

"Just West?"

"Yep."

"West's a hell of a direction to be headed in if you ain't got a idea where you're headed in it. You going to Omaha?"

Cyrus chews his ham. "I have thought some on Omaha."

"You got to be hellbent to go anywhere west of there."

"Well, sir," Cyrus says, "I am hellbent. I will give you that."

The smith nods, almost sadly. Turns to Galina. "Hard riding, ma'am?"

"Can be. We don't often meet with kindness on the road."

"Well. You're welcome to it. Can get plenty lonesome of a evening here. I am glad you are here."

"So are the both of us."

"Yes. Yes, of course."

The smith asks Cyrus a few questions about their mounts which demonstrate great ignorance of horses and the talk soon dries up. Outside a stage rumbles past under heavy escort. There's always a reason someone pays good coin for an escort and Cyrus wonders what it is in this case. The smith fixes up hammocks for the pair. Rain lashes the smithy and it seems a great luxury to sleep inside again. Cyrus sleeps well for the smith has nothing worth the taking and so no plans are required.

—§—

Cyrus wakes to see the smith staggering from the hearth, hand jammed to his throat leaking vital fluids. Cyrus leaps from the hammock, grabs a heavy iron bar, brains the smith. When he is prone Cyrus gives him a few more wallops. He and Galina stand over him cold footed.

"You didn't hear him coming at me?" says Galina, holding a blooded penknife.

"Shit," he says. "You ought to keep me in your loop some, woman."

"I thought I did."

Cyrus spits. "Son of a bitch ran his yap too much anyhow."

At dawn Galina finds a new pair of women's riding breeches in a sappy pine box. She pulls them on and asks if it is true, if they are bound for Omaha.

"Like I said," says Cyrus. "I thought on it some. I ain't ever got a straight shot in this country."

"Anyone coming after you? For them straight shots you never got?"

He looks at her sharply. "They ain't doing much of a job if they are."

"So Omaha. Then what?"

"West."

"Why?"

"I was born out west. Pa died in the Harrows when I was still a squirt and we hoofed it back east like everyone else. Now I'm headed west to get back what's mine."

—§—

In the gathering chill, they ride on a week, two. The road consists of frigid mud and they pass shuffling processions of pilgrims bound for hand-built shrines to the Virgin Mary. They come to an earthworks where snaking lines of coolies quarry rock from a wasteland of bracken and swamp to fortify a settlement up the valley. The whips of the taskmasters sing from mules to men. Cyrus and Galina halt when a sledge hefted by twenty mules and piled thirty hands high with rock slowly crosses their path. An overseer approaches with a bullwhip half uncoiled.

"You looking for work?" he says.

"Not no work of this kind," says Cyrus.

"You well-set, are you?"

"Well enough."

The taskmaster lowers the bullwhip. "I envy you for it. We ain't had a dram of comfort or the tallow to see it by in weeks. Ain't none of us ... begging your pardon ma'am, but you're the first real woman I seen in two months. But we all of us got our duty, don't we?"

"Shit," Cyrus says.

The land beyond the earthworks runs to ruined farmland, abandoned and burned. At the head of the valley is the settlement, ringed by trenches where more coolies dump rocks for a bulwarks which serves no purpose Cyrus or Galina can see. The only public building is a brothel.

"A drink ain't going to kill me," says Cyrus. "You want to wait out here?"

"I'm going with you," says Galina.

"Suit yourself."

A bevy of tarts strut among the tables inside. Cyrus quaffs whiskys till woozy and does not resist a plump redhead tart who bares a breast and palms his thigh.

"Who's that?" the tart says, eyeing Galina.

"Someone I know," says Cyrus.

"She comes along, it's extra," says the tart.

"All right," says Cyrus.

A drunken merchant with waxed and twirled mustache comes and sits swaying next to Galina.

"You don't look like the rest of these sluts," he says. "You look like something special. How about it? You something special?"

"I'd watch yourself," says Cyrus.

"You watch your own self," says the merchant. "I know how to handle a wench."

"All right," says Cyrus.

"Buy me a brandy," says Galina.

The merchant does, hand cocked over Galina's thigh. She polishes off the brandy and before the merchant can so much as curl fingers round his own glass, she has out her penknife and he goes twitching on the floor.

"We better get upstairs, honey," says the tart.

"Aye," says Cyrus. "We best."

Cyrus takes a suite with private jakes, a novelty to him. He remains inside a long time and in the bedroom the tart and Galina hear splashing. He has left the coin purse on a lamp stand. The tart sits naked on the edge of the bed chewing a plug of tobacco, olive bruises about her mouth. Galina sits in a chair looking out the window at the guttering lights of the settlement.

"What do you say, honey?" says the tart.

"About what?" says Galina.

"About that," says the tart, pointing at the pouch. "Go halvsies with you."

"What about him?"

"Don't you worry bout him."

The tart squats over her shed dress and removes a packet of powder from an inner pocket. She empties the contents into the whisky on the lamp stand. After a while Cyrus returns shirtless. The tart lays him flat on the bed and removes his boots, juggling her pasty ass in his face. Then she straddles him and offers the whisky.

"You need some relaxing," the tart says.

Galina stands and brains the tart with the iron doorstop. The tart flops like a boneless chicken to the floor.

"Didn't take you for a jealous one," says Cyrus.

"She medicined it up," says Galina.

"Did she now," Cyrus says. He goes downstairs and gets himself conducted to the proprietor's office.

"You didn't kill her, did you?" says the proprietor, dressed in a three-piece suit and flanked by guards who stand with hands loose at their sides.

"Naw. I fell in love with her."

The proprietor guffaws. "Well, I don't believe you can afford her contract."

"I believe I can," says Cyrus. "How much?"

"Two hundred dollars."

"Ain't no woman alive worth half that much and no whore worth half that. I'll give you fifty."

"One seventy-five."

"Sixty," says Cyrus, and counts out the coins on the proprietor's desk.

They take the tart wrapped in a dressing gown out the back stairway down to the narrow lane rank with sewage. She cannot keep her feet and mutters gibberish. Cyrus lashes the tart to Galina's stallion. Then they ride through the night back to the earthworks, Cyrus and Galina double mounted on Drue. The overseer is in a shack huddled round a brazier with his fellows. Cyrus undoes the knots and lets the tart slide into the mud where she stares stupidly up at the men.

"My compliments," says Cyrus.

"Thank you, sir," says the overseer, running fingers through his hair. "Thank you sure."

"Make good use of her now."

"We will, sir, we will."

The pair have not gone unmarked and passing back through the settlement are set upon by a gang of hooded men. Cyrus is knocked from Drue and robbed of funds and six-shooter once more. The hooded men do not pursue Galina galloping away on a stallion.

When she circles back Galina follows the bloody smear in the mud to where Cyrus has dragged himself under a tree. Drue stands over him. She helps him mount, straps his hands to the saddle horn. Takes up the stallion's reins and leading along Drue, continues west.

MOONDOG OVER THE MEKONG

ไปเข้ามาในชีวิตใหม่

—1—

She came from a Lao village deep in the countryside where the crops failed for three consecutive years and an agent placed a season's income in cash on the floor mat in her family home, with the promise of thrice that and much more after her parents bonded her over. He came from a city in America, across a great expanse of land and water, a new man come to a new country, having effected a clean escape from the old, as completely gone from his old life as a range-crossing cowboy.

She arrived at the karaoke shack ringed with Christmas lights by a longtail boat, which brought her over the Mekong into Thailand under cover of darkness, following a two-day journey by bus, a rickety contraption of Soviet make that rattled over deeply-pocked roads, after a full day standing with twenty-five others in the back of a pickup from a small town, reached by a day in a buffalo-drawn cart from her village, she who'd never been more than a half day's walk from home; she cried the whole first day she was there, after the mamasan made her job description clear.

In the old days, he could've hired on a ship with no more asked of him than his name, sinking out of sight of his homeland forever; but in these mistrustful latter days, knowing his every move could be effortlessly tracked, it was necessary to construct an alternative identity; so, with a few fraudulent facts and a PO Box, he commenced to fill out forms, taking extreme care not to overlap his life as a Commercial Loan Officer at the Bank of Milwaukee, married (no children), homeowner, car owner, vacations to the Dells and Acapulco, baseball fan, in casual shape; watching with pleasure as helpful websites constructed an alter ego with predilections he'd previously only dreamed at: single, renter, user of public transportation, excursions to the Rockies and Sierra Nevadas, participant in individual endurance sports, in excellent shape.

She was still blubbering when her first client casually removed his pants in a bamboo shack, to run howling out of the shack a moment later wearing only a T-shirt, clutching his crotch where she'd twisted with the same dexterous force she used to decollate chickens back in the village, provoking peals of laughter from his companions and a furious mamasan to beat her with the bamboo rod till her tear ducts went dry, after which she was locked for three days in a back shack formerly used to house laying hens, dusty with piles of dried shit swarming with scurrying insects, not enough room to stand up or lay down, the mamasan peeking in every few hours to prod and poke with the rod, and when she was let out, the other girls, Lao imports all and which she called "sisters," washed her and cooed at her gently not to be a fool, and she did not resist her second client, a ship hand who took her virginity with great bemusement, wiping off the blood on her shirt; he was on his lunch break, in a seedy side street, renting out an upstairs room in a vast mansion transformed into a tenement house where no questions were asked, for use in storing the material effects – passport, driver's license, clothes, traveling gear, credit cards, and so forth – necessary to make good his escape.

The following morning, as she absent-mindedly massaged the hurt between her legs, squatting by the cooking fire and staring off to the east and home, she let the soup boil over; the mamasan smacked her upside the head with the rod, hissing that she best pay attention if she didn't want a daily beating, which the mamasan would nevertheless happily administer, he was with his wife, attending the final couples therapy session, the therapist saying they ought really to continue the therapy, especially him, who needed much work to expose and treat the root of his problems accepting the responsibilities of mature adult life, but nonetheless, in the therapist's professional opinion, they were on a sound footing and should enjoy many years of marital harmony and companionship.

A week later, as he was cashing out nine years of earnings on his pension fund, ostensibly to re-invest it in a market with higher returns, against the staid advice of the Chief Loan Officer, who considered it an irresponsible thing for a man well within child-rearing years to do, placing the lions share in his wife's personal account, where it would not be visible until the following month's statement, converting the rest into trackless traveler's checks which he left with an icy thrill inside a desk drawer in the rented room, thus completing the secret series of financial transactions that ensured he'd be well-supplied with ready cash while leaving his wife in possession of their material property and assets, a client hit her hard enough to loosen a molar when she was unable to make his cock stiffen even slightly, despite trying every trick her sisters had taught her; the bouncer, who swung on a cot with half-hooded eyes outside the karaoke shack and spoke only in grunts, heard her screams and burst in, beating the client senseless with a tire iron, until his buddies silently drug the man off into the night, trailing blood into the dust, causing the karaoke shack to empty of clients, for which the mamasan beat her with the rod until she couldn't even whimper.

He was on a transpacific flight six days later, new identity a roaring success, divested of all possessions beyond the plane, watching bad movies on a distant screen and drinking Bloody Marys, which he was surprised to learn were free, as she limped down to the riverbank, just able to walk again after long days curled up in a sleeping hut, trying to get command of mutinous limbs and sinews and muscles in the afternoon heat, looking towards home across the gray dull-shimmering water that coursed sluggishly between rocky banks, gently rocking the hollow-bumping longtail boats tied to the bank, and down the Thai side, she saw hunched-over peasants tending vegetable patches that sloped up to the river promenade of the nearby town, where she could make out bare-legged strollers with ice cream cones under the shade of banyan trees – in the village they would be rounding up rice seedlings and butchering dogs, and her heart quivered wondering when she'd see home again, but, knowing she was paying for the seedlings and dogs this year, she went, weak as an arthritic old woman, back up to the karaoke shack, where her dim-lit nights were busy, pouring beer over ice for grubby Thai and Lao clients who warbled badly at the karaoke machine and after sufficient beer, took her to the one of the bamboo shacks behind the tin karaoke shack, and climbed on her to finish what they'd begun with groping at the table, sometimes one a night, sometimes several, as on the night he touched down in Bangkok, wet air sticking his shirt to his back, half-drunk and half-hungover; blinking under the yellow sodium lights underneath the expressway, a man with a black suit and a Mercedes took him to his hotel, requiring what seemed an exorbitant lot of bills for the service, where he toppled into his twenty-third story bed, repeating his new name to himself, that he might not forget in this new land.

A few days later, a Thai trader took her out of the karaoke shack, after handing the mamasan a stack of bills palmed too quickly for her to count, as he hit the dusty red road of the wide-plained countryside that curved out into the gauzy horizon lined with leaned-over palm trees and stilted huts and tendrils of smoke, driving a rented jeep guardedly on the opposite side of the road across scorched dry-season rice paddies, weaving through aimlessly shepherded herds of water buffalo and slat ribbed cattle, talking with a circle of monks at a dusty temple with a serene Buddha in a boat, eating sticky rice and speaking the badly broken Thai he'd gotten from a boxed language course (practiced in that solitary room), while the trader locked her in a backroom of a warehouse, where workers made use of her two dozen times daily for a week on a floor mattress; she was fed rice and curried fish and did not leave the room, sickly rays of sun filtering through the grimed-over window over the crumpled pile of clothes and underwear she didn't bother to put back on, never knowing when the next one might show up, as he swam in a muddy pond and shrieking village children poked and prodded at his flaccid skin, then at the headman's house he sat on a floor mat scooping up unrecognizable globs of food so spicy his eyes watered in steady streams, passing around Marlboro cigarettes and a bottle of Jack Daniels, the dozen men there quickly polishing off the bottle, everyone grinning at everyone, before falling asleep outdoors just after sunfall, waking at dawn to discover a column of tiny black ants running up his leg; he bathed in the pond and headed down another red back road, as the Thai trader brought her back to the karaoke shack, where she collapsed into a dead sleep for a day and a half, after which her pubic hair was so gummy and matted that her sisters advised her to shave it off; besides, they said, tiny as she was, clients would like it, so she did, thereafter saving herself a good deal of chafing.

On northeastwards he went, disregarding roadmaps, knowing eventually he would come to the Mekong, which he'd settled on in the rented room to give some substance to his voyage, liking the two syllables tripping exotically off his tongue; he carefully tacked up a Lands Of The Mekong wall map, and found that, for all the thousands of miles the river flowed through six countries, the only reasonable access point was Bangkok, which required a long traverse of countryside that he'd greedily anticipated and now greedily took in, as she discovered that large gulps of beer were magic: first swimming cold fire in her stomach, then mystifying numbness in her lips, finally delightful lightness in her head, making the coarse client across the table almost handsome and nearly amusing and sometimes she could pretty well ignore his frenzied thrustings later; at first the mamasan approved of this gambit, offering all the girls two bahts' incentive for every beer they got emptied, to which the girls responded with sudden clumsiness, spilling an inordinate number and pouring extras out, ruses the mamasan responded to by culling a week's pay from each girl, with twenty strokes of the rod for her, who the mamasan blamed for causing the foolishness in the first place.

A great bank of thunderclouds rushed over the Lao jungle onto the Thai rice plains, lashing the earth with sideways sheets of rain.

Fearful of storm spirits, she cowered in the karaoke shack with her sisters as the storm raged outside, kept company by chickens, a buffalo who breathed heavily and deposited clumps of steaming shit, and some dogs which she eyed hungrily as lunchtime passed and no one was willing to leave the warm group to cook in back, rain finally slackening as it grew dark, thunder fading to distant rumbling, lightning still peppering the sky and lighting up the wide spine of the river.

He left the jeep top down and drove on as the storm hit, whooping as the rain washed over him like a baptism, following the headlights through rain-reflected air, down a road that dipped and disappeared beneath torrents that nearly reached the engine block before climbing to gray vistas of warm downpour, landscape cloaked behind silver curtains, reaching a town where the road gave out, climbing out as the rain misted over to a sprinkle, wondering where he was, until dancing lightning lit up fast-gone flashes of the great river below and the land beyond, marveling to think how far he'd come; he drank beer on the river promenade, practicing Thai phrases from a damp textbook, stumbling back to his bungalow as the last of the lightning ebbed away, knocking over bottles as the amused Thai staff watched from a polite distance.

The next day she was scrubbing shit stains off the cement floor of the karaoke shack and washing her work outfits – two miniskirts, two spaghetti-strap tops – wondering if the seedlings were in the paddies and if she'd be home by harvest, as he was wandering the town half a mile away, smiling at locals who smiled back broadly and tossed English phrases ("Where you go?" "You come from?") at him, taking a trail that led to cliff paintings etched by unknown tribes millennia ago, shapes of fish and fire and human hands, and he sat on the dusty trail in the midday heat looking up at them, flushed with instinctual certainty bubbling up in his veins that he had been here before, had played a part in creating these etchings, the instinct laying latent in untold generations of genes until summoned forth by the sight, until a waxy insect dangerously resembling a wasp alighted on his arm, and standing with a stumble to shake it off, the feeling vanished; he walked back to town certain he would never go home.

That evening, as she put on a miniskirt and T-shirt, brushed out her hair, and sat with the youngest sister outside the karaoke shack, he was drinking more beer and practicing more phrases draped in solitude at the same promenade restaurant, while the Christmas lights flicked on and she swatted at mosquitoes and no clients came.

But it was early. She waited.

He had more beer watching timid local couples court along the promenade, wooing in gentle tones and without touching but more obviously needful of each other than he had ever been of anyone, twin daggers of envy and loneliness stabbing him, the couples taking no notice of him walking slowly past to the jeep, thinking a drive might clear his head; he followed a road which trailed alongside the river out of town, thoughts of happy couples keeping his foot on the accelerator, until there were sudden sharp beams in his eyes and shadowy figures motioning him to pull over; she idly nudged a dozing dog and speculated at the pleasing thought that this could be a night when she had no clients; any stragglers would be scarfed up by the older sisters, and she could stay outside with the youngest sister, and no one would sweat on her.

"You, where you go?" said a cop, blinding him with a flashlight and flanked by two others. Noticing their pistols and wide unchanging smiles, he felt no menace in their voices or pose, but a cold surety something was required of him.

"I'm driving," he said. "Just driving."

The cop said, "Okay, okay. You drive. You see. Okay. Take cash."

Through the cop's thick accent, he might've heard "pass," as in "passport"; "What?" he said.

The cop said, "Cash. Money. Baht. Cash."

No guesswork this time, so he handed over a few hundred-baht bills, which the cop folded deftly into a breast pocket with a free hand.

"Okay, okay," the cop said, and waved him on.

Down the pothole-festooned road, which veered sharply to the left, he stopped, jeep idling in fumy burbles, eyeing the murk beyond the pallid halogen pools of his flickering headlights. His skin was electric, something in the air permeating the row of shacks outlined by blinking Christmas lights, shadowy figures around them, so he jerkily engaged the clutch, feeling he must do anything but act suspicious, as though he'd coolly done this hundreds of times, driven into the dark night to park up a steep upslope in front of the second shack on the right, bathed in reality and thinking there was no reason ever to go back anywhere, headlights beaming onto two girls sitting outside with legs demurely crossed, eyes flashing silver.

The headlights blinded her like always, but, trained by rod strokes not to shield her eyes, she smiled, not moving from her perch, to allow the client to go inside for an older sister to make overtures at, which only the most brazen client would decline, to his great detriment, as the sulky rejected sister would instruct her replacement to treat the usurper poorly, a practice the mamasan had failed to stamp out, since the older sisters contemptuously stared down the upraised rod, leaving the mamasan hissing threats and muttering in the cooking area, fearful for the solvency that rested in their skillful ministrations, so the rod, needing somewhere to fall, would end on the younger sisters; and then the lights cut out, and getting out of the jeep was the last thing in all the world she could've expected: a *boxida*, a foreigner, tall pasty man with slightly bulging belly and dark hair and clean white arms with fingernails that caught the gleam of the Christmas lights as he went with a conquering stride inside, eyes running over her small frame, and she, too surprised to even look away, caught his scent, deep and musky and speaking of warmth in cold places, having before only seen flickering TV images of boxida, who, it was said, existed in numberless hordes in faraway places cold enough to crack bones, ruling the world from palaces of ice, their strange angular symbols imprinted on the very clothes she wore, their power greater than even the spirits; he went inside to shuffling and laughing and breaking glass and she abandoned her post, because she could not miss the chance to see a boxida with her own eyeballs.

She was the first thing he saw, and though old conditioning urged a retreat to what now seemed the safe-as-home haven of his bungalow, much older urges kept him moving forward, the girl as lovely as any coaxed by mad dreams from a feverish brain, skin so dark it blended in a smooth ridge into her shadow, eyes onyx as an abyss, face as fine-ridged as fired porcelain; inside were tables ringed by molded plastic chairs, a karaoke machine that resembled a jukebox from his childhood, the kind with actual records inside, and receiving no welcomes or directions from the group of girls gathered in the corner, giggling and gabbling and slack-jawed staring like the villagers he'd encountered, he sat down in a corner, quaking but alive as fire.

Her strong sisters, able to resist the mamasan, were unwilling to approach the boxida, who might herald sick horrors or drink their young blood, so before she could summon courage or thought, she sat down across from him, back to her sisters, looking in his face, her only defense a smile so broad her back molars gleamed, as long seconds slid forward with the most bated of expectations on both sides, hush reverberating from her sisters behind; he drummed his fingers on the table and, in a voice deep-rumbly as yesterday's thunder, pronounced a sound that must have passed for a word among his people, the shack going dead silent, no one sure what he could want, until he curled his fingers around an imaginary glass and put it to his mouth, causing great peals of laughter among the sisters, and when the boxida said the word again, she caught a muted echo of the language spoken here across the river, and the word was, "Drink?"

"Drink," she repeated, standing up, knocking her knees against the table and nearly falling over, a smile rising on his creased face like a creature from the murky deep, white and dark at the same time, and crossing the uneven cement floor for beer, she tried to ignore her sisters, gazing at her in wide wonder while trying to pretend all was normal, that they were as used to seeing boxida as they were to picking the plumpest crickets out of the supper pail, the mamasan peeping in from the back doorway, wondering if what she'd heard was true, that you could reap enormous profits off boxida, and glad that should the boxida prove to be the blood-drinker of village legend, the casualty would be the shack's least-valued hand, that sniveling bitch so stoic beneath her blows; she brought over four cans of beers and a pail full of ice, not re-eyeing him as she plunked ice in the glasses and poured it over the beer, and they clinked glasses, she still not looking up but unable to stop the smile furrowing her face. They drank.

A sister got a song going; over the loud music, in patchy phrases and long silences, surreptitiously studying each other's faces, the two worked out that he spoke no Lao and she spoke no English, but they had enough Thai between them for the basics: names, citizenship, ages, confirmation of eye colors, a mutual lack of Thai singing ability, compliments on looks (which she could not believe he meant), mutual affection for beer (both drinking too fast), a comparison of hand sizes (a sharp thrill running up his arm to touch of her silken skin); and then, beer gone, she said, "Go?"

He wasn't sure why she was ready to go, or what they'd do once gone, but eyeing over her beauty once more and bucked up with raw reality and liquid courage, he said, "Okay."

She scribbled a number on a damp napkin and slid it across the table; new realities dawning on him, he accepted with a nod, barely reading the digit, handing some bills over, heart jigging wildly at the thought of lines-never-to-be-uncrossed and a sweat-sudden fear that this was an elaborate setup, and any moment cops would burst in, clap him in handcuffs, and take him to a stinking solitary cell somewhere in the monkey-howling jungle, here where no one even imagined he existed, while she gave over the shack's share to the mamasan, who endeavored to see how much the little girl kept for herself, but she kept the bills tightly palmed, and then returned to him, where they drank their dregs, (older sisters observing every movement), and went to the jeep, he shivering from bowels to crown – he'd never done anything of this sort even in dreams, or been so bewitched by a woman's lithe animal-grace, but he tried to show nothing, and she followed him out slump-shouldered and silent, not looking back at her sisters, though she wasn't quite sure she would ever see them again.

He got in the jeep and fumbled with the keys, dropping them twice, pawing for the ignition through a haze, senses muffled in cottony stupor, as she watched, lacking any of the prerequisites necessary to form judgments, all the reference points of all her previous life washed away; he got the jeep going and they backed over the rain ruts down the slope, headlights reflecting the dull green eyes of the languid buffalo, turning left and then right, past the checkpoint, cops lounging on ubiquitous plastic chairs, into town, and he relaxed somewhat as they neared the bungalow: as yet he'd committed no crime, as she gripped the door handle in a fierce try for calm, realizing the only one who could bring her back to anything she knew was the one who'd taken her out of it.

Parking with front wheels on the river promenade, the spot he'd left less than an hour earlier, he was working on forgetting the transaction that'd brought her here, so it seemed uncouth to take her straight to the bungalow; she followed him to the promenade railing, water diamond white under a plump moon daubed by wispy clouds, encircled by a silken halo, the moon walking a moondog, reminding him of the pre-superstore vacant lot behind his childhood subdivision, last refuge of the fireflies, where they played on warm nights, the only place he remembered noticing a moondog before, which to her was a good omen, since the moon, that giver of false light to nefarious spirits and vicious animals, only became docile when accompanied by the kind spirit of a gentle white dog, a comforting pale like his skin, here in this place where she was uncertain of the very ground, suffused in dappled alabastrine light that sharpened outlines while obscuring details, of the forest across the river, of the boats rocking in the river below, of each other's faces, which they watched each other watching for the first time.

"A moondog," he said, in his language.

"A moondog," she said, in hers.

Each understood, somehow, and he stroked her arm, soft as moonlight to touch, and she leaned against him, and they watched the moondog walk.

—2—

She was like no woman he'd known: sensuous as glossed silk, acrobatic and unashamed, bringing him to three more acts than he thought himself capable of in a single night and after she melded into him as though created for this sole purpose, concaving into his contours with a gentle sturdiness that somehow bespoke a lifelong intention to have been there always, as though not only all his life had been preparation for this day, but hers also; which was not so far from the truth as he thought, since she knew boxida to be capable of anything from blood-drinking to whisking you away to a great gleaming city, filled with hairy pale-bodies, so far beyond the forests and rice paddies nobody in living memory had seen one, where machines did the work of men, animals were slaughtered in great killing-machines, all were rich and happy though there were no trees, disease and evil spirits were banished (the village shaman saying this was why the spirits had grown cruel – so many sought revenge for being expelled), and to be alone with a boxida was to have a chance at an untold reality beyond all previous possibility; unbuckling his belt she readied herself for anything, but she found the usual equipment, though unhealthily sallow, and the fucking was nearly the same, the boxida capable of less go-arounds than her usual all-nighter, which was delightful; what was truly different came after, when she lay back with a delicious sinking sensation on a bed too soft to be believed, crinkly white sheets cleaner than the rain, and in the bathroom, rather than scooping a few handfuls of fetid water between her legs (normally all the cleanup she was allowed while an impatient client smoked outside), she stood under placid streams of water warm as the sun, together with him, kind boxida, towering wider than two of her, who rubbed soap (so sweet-smelling she almost gagged) on her belly and breasts and between her shoulder blades, hands supple as trod-over mud, which kept on touching and touching and touching, even where she made her trade, without wanting to fuck, only to touch, and she liked it, the first hands she could remember that caressed her with affection, and in the bathroom's bright light, she got a clear look in his eyes, great, deep, green, her reflection clear in them; by the time he handed her a velvety towel, maybe the kindest material she'd ever touched, she was so dizzingly overawed she barely knew she was in love with this boxida, more godlike and more human than anyone she'd known in her eighteen years; after the shower he stroked her head – so light! – and she was already asleep, body warm to the touch as she exhaled warm pools of air on his chest, and all his previous life seemed a dream, one that melts before the reality of a new room it takes you a moment to recognize waking up, and though he'd come seeking only a sight of the Mekong, he felt sure he'd found what all men seek.

In the morning, they awoke somewhat staggered to each other's presence, athletically made love and had another shower, then walked to the market, fingers touching shyly, him oblivious and she forcedly indifferent to the gawks of the stall owners and shoppers, bringing back egg-battered rice cakes, greasy fried bread, and coffee, eating at the table in front of the bungalow as morning birds wheeled and cackled over the gray-flowing Mekong; he decided he could not part from her if it meant leaving her undefended in that ratty shack, and she, as yet prosaic, was keeping her hopes to a large tip, to put with the stash she'd managed to hide away, half a hundred dollars worth of Thai and Lao currency in a small cloth wallet tied around her waist. She shivered in the morning breeze and he ran back to the market, buying her two oversized sweatshirts with superstore brand names from worlds ago; she put one on and with the other covered her legs, which seemed ridiculously exposed in her miniskirt to morning air and staring eyes, watching carefully as the boxida, her boxida, ate in much the same manner as he drank beer the night before, which is to say, as people did, though it would not have surprised her if secret mandibles unfolded from his head to deposit food into a gullet in his back, but he remained human, even as his deep green eyes were godlike.

Finished, the day stretched out before them, and she knew that, boxida or no boxida, she'd best get back, before the mamasan took exception to a too-long absence, since her normal stock in trade, not liking to mix the businesses of day and night, always had her back by dawn, where she cleaned the shack and then made lunch with the youngest sisters for the others, and during the long idle afternoons, though homesickness was a deep daily gutache, she sometimes thought her lot was not so bad – back in the village the labor was ceaseless, hanging over your head even when you were working, the incessant cycles that kept food in stomachs and clothes on backs and rice in the paddies and the next generation coming along, whereas here, when the mamasan didn't beat her (a thing her own mother had not spared her, at that) and as long as she stayed in the good graces of the older sisters and kept her mind off the coming night, life was good enough, and she sent back vaster sums to the village than her family could possibly know what to do with, though she knew it would all be gone when she returned – and now here was a miraculous karmic contortion, a boxida who'd liberated her from her reality for a night, and in the stout circle of his arms she was positive even the most malevolent of spirits could not harm her. But how could he have any use for her now, beyond the one he'd already satisfied?

"Where you want to go?" he asked, his accent making his voice sound like an underwater breeze.

"Back," she said, her voice a warbling singsong to him, but taking in the meaning, his expression dropped so precipitously, like a child seeing its father beat up on a public thoroughfare, that she ran a finger across his clenched knuckles and said, "Just to see mamasan. Must see her."

"And then?" he asked. "You go with me?"

Her heart swelled at the thought, but what would the mamasan say, but, "Yes," she said. "I go with you."

At the checkpoint were different cops, looking less authoritative in morning's inclined yellow light; having already heard a foreigner quick with the cash had passed by last night, they affably received documentation in currency; a left, a right, then he was weaving around the buffalo standing in front of the karaoke shack, brakes squeaking with road dust, killing the engine and waiting in the driver's seat as instructed. She went inside, past the bouncer dozing on one of the tables, back to the cooking area where the mamasan was squatting by the fire with the two older sisters, eating rice porridge and examining a pailful of palm-sized water bugs still wet from forest ponds.

She said to the mamasan, "He wants me to go with him."

"Cost him a pretty penny," said the mamasan, not looking up from the water bugs she was prodding with a forefinger. "For how long?"

"Today," she said. "Tonight."

"Did he hurt you? Did he go after your blood?" asked the first sister.

"Oh no. He was, oh, so nice," she said, reeling with memory and lacking words, nothing in her experience having prepared her to describe such an experience, though it seemed natural as wet-season floods.

"A blood-sucker with cash," said the second sister. "How much you get out of him?"

"Enough," she said.

"He best have plenty more where that came from," said the mamasan, looking at her cheeks, oily soft with the white lotion he'd daubed on them that morning. "You can talk to him okay?"

"He doesn't talk like us. He talks like they do over here."

"Well, you can talk that. Even stupid as you are, I bet you've learned that much since I rescued you from the mud. Tell him it's three thousand a day."

There was silence at this shocking sum: twenty go-arounds in the bamboo shacks. A stick popped and cracked in the fire.

"That's for me, mind you," said the mamasan. "Whatever else you can get is between you and him. And you best keep track of it, because I'll be needing a third of that. Half."

He'd paid five times the going rate last night, so she thought he'd pay – it was far far more than she'd ever gotten before, but still dizzy from the night, she could hardly think of money, which would disappear anyhow, down the craw of the mamasan or the village.

"Okay," she said, going to get some clothes, not liking him waiting, forgetting her sisters, who were not forgetting, the mamasan not liking this little girl so suddenly uninhibited, who hadn't even bothered to bargain like a respectable person, fearing loss of control if she gave the little girl free rein in full view of the other girls, who'd thenceforth spend their time plotting similar escapes. The mamasan flipped a water bug onto its back, legs flailing slowly as she kept a finger on its thorax, almost ready for the eating, primed like the profit the little girl'd bring her from the puffy boxida, but, like the water bug, the little girl would go bitter if let grow too big; she came back in street clothes.

"You can't stay away from here long, you know," the mamasan said. "The police catch you, they'll beat the boxida right out of you. And don't think I'm going to let you come crawling back here with no teeth."

"Like as not he'll suck you dry in your sleep," said the first sister.

"Make sure he keeps the cash flowing," said the second sister.

She looked at them, swimming in a haze only her boxida could clear, only the being next to him; she was down deep in a vortex, and had no desire to resist; she said nothing and headed outside, where he was waiting in the mounting mid-morning heat, fearful at each second of her absence of horrors swallowing her like a venus fly-trap, and incredulous there was no long line of men like him – drawing on to middle age, broken, lost, fitful, terrified of hope – waiting for dark gossamer angels to emerge from tin shacks perched between dry jungle and rasping river, why men everywhere were not seeking what he'd stumbled across, promise of happiness so cheaply purchased; he might just as easily have driven past this town, or never gotten on the plane, or never watched his wife become a stranger, or watched his life turn alien around his Loan Officer's desk, and so missed everything. There she was, black hair sparkling fine as fairy dust, and then she was beside him, and she was thinking, Beside him nothing bad can happen, he is beyond the realm of troubles, and with him, I am also, all of everything is forever changed now.

Through the gauntlet of head-tilted stares in town, they went back to the bungalow, not leaving that day or night, ordering in food, saturating towels and ruining bed sheets. He lost all interest in the country beyond the bungalow door, ceaselessly retreading the small landscape of the new country in bed with him, while she forgot all of her place in the world in the wonder of his strong grip, and both ignored tomorrow's inevitable approach.

When morning came, he was still lost, but her head flooded with thoughts of fearsome Thai police with long spiked clubs and the money the mamasan held for her family, who would be running through their last food reserves, afraid of angering her boxida by speaking of her troubles, by asking if he could get money across the river and hundreds of kilometers upcountry to her family, instead of giving it to her.

"Go back?" he said, not quite believing she wanted to go, not quite believing he'd take her.

"Back. Must go back. See mamasan. Maybe you pay again, we come back here again."

Desperate to get at every detail of her existence prior to him, he'd asked everything his overtaxed Thai vocabulary allowed, questions she answered as well as she was able, about her family, motley coterie of relatives relying on her for survival; which sent a sickening chill of delight through him, since it meant he'd found her in that squalid shack through no choice of her own, and already thinking to supply all the cash they could need; but she said nothing, so he consented, feeling he could do nothing else, and they went back through the checkpoint, official outlay the same (his face well-remembered), and again she disappeared inside the shack, and again he sweated under the morning sun.

Inside, the first sister, braiding her hair at a mirror propped up on the karaoke machine, bruised and sore from the three ship hands who'd trained her in the bamboo shacks last night, after securing a group discount, out of which the mamasan refused to lessen the shack's share, turned to her and said, "Back from pretty-pretty-land, are you? Hope you're not starting to think there's no work for you here."

"Oh, no," she said, brushing by to the back, where the mamasan was squatting alone.

She said, "He wanted to bring me back here. To make sure?"

"Of what?" said the mamasan.

"That I can go with him again. He wants ... "

"That all you can think about? What he wants? Is he the one putting rice on the mat back at home? Is he the one who took your sin-black body in, gave you a home, gave you a chance at more money than you're like to see the rest of your reeking paddy-trodding life? Is he?"

"No," she said, not looking at the mamasan, her family waiting on that money, and if the mamasan kept it, and what could she do, what could he do?

"And your sisters. You think you can go traipsing around the country with some fat boxida, leaving them all the work? Just last night we had to turn clients away. What happens when word spreads about that? Your boxida will be back in boxida-land with his wife, you'll be out in the mud, this place turns to nothing. What happens to me, little girl?"

Outside he would be waiting, getting hot, oh, he got so hot so quickly, he couldn't take the sun, he said the sun was not the same in boxida-land, not burning like here where you had to hide in the shade, in boxida-land, he said, people had pale skin and blinding green eyes like his and everyone drove cars and it was bigger than ten trips back and forth to her village, and there was snow, white as clouds and colder than ice, which she'd seen on TV but never believed in, and she'd asked him, more than once, if he had a wife in boxida-land, and he said over and over the only one he could think of was her, and she believed him with all her small strength, and for her, too, there was only him – which didn't mean there wasn't her family, and she didn't know the way home, the agent did all the talking and ticket-buying, but she was sure she could find the way with him, but then, what of the money she'd endured these long months to get, swallowing acts that would've made an outcast of her at home, but whose performance here preserved that very home; if she ran, she might as well light a match to that money meant for them, because her family would never see it, and everything would have been for nothing, but, oh, her boxida was waiting.

"You mean ...?" she said.

"I mean, get back in here where you belong. Nice up to your sisters. Tell him to go away."

"He'll pay, mamasan. However much you want. Don't make him go."

This was the mamasan's knife-edged dilemma, and she was incensed the little girl was pressing her thumb on it. She'd heard the stories. Those stories, of pale-faced boxida who threw money around like the paper they wiped their asses with (not that she believed any people anywhere, even blood-drinkers, would do something so filthy), slow-moving as giant geckos, requiring only a smile to trap, but always they went back to boxida-land, and what was she left with then, if she let the shack fall around her head for one of them? Her clients, they wouldn't like it, would they, if word got round that she was toadying up to foreigners, they'd talk in vile voices in other shacks about how she'd gotten uppity, jacking up prices and pandering to pale-bodies who laughed at her, and she'd wake up one morning to find everything gone: for one little girl and a boxida. No, she'd made up her mind overnight, as the other girls grumbled in the background. If she let him get his pasty claws any more deeply into the little girl, this boxida was going to cost her more than she could ever make off him, and though her rough fingers clenched in rage to think of the thousands she was throwing away, there was no choice.

"Away," the girl choked out.

"For good. Tell him whatever you have to. He'll go. You'll see. You best work some more cash off of him, because it's your last chance. And then get your skinny black ass back in here. There's work for you."

What could she do, unable to think, barely able to walk, out to the jeep, where he was waiting and smiling, looking at her as no one had ever done, love and worship on his face, feeling herself unworthy, even as a crooked candle of hope sputtered in a dark corner of her mind that maybe she could be, and what she wanted was to jump into the jeep and go spinning off into the future, he'd know what to do, where to go, he knew everything, but, touching his outstretched hand on the driver's side, she said, "Must go back. Must work here. You go away."

He eyed her carefully, searching for a promising secret in her words, finding none, crushing reminder of how ignorant he was of how things ran here, of what he might be stomping his clumsy foot into, of how he might unwittingly be hurting her: he'd been in this country, on this continent, less than three weeks and at her side less than thirty-six hours, hours as shining real as any he could recall, slimy sheen of unreality painted over all the years and places and people before her, standing small beside the jeep, pulling her small soft gentle hand out of his, stepping back, stepping away.

"I come tonight," he said. "Okay?"

"Cannot," she said. "Mamasan, she say you cannot."

Only one form of work here, thought revolting as death, her being handled – rented! – by other men, dirty hateful men; he said, "No. I come tonight. To see you. Must see you."

"Cannot," she said, and backed up a couple more steps, heart bashing out cavities on the inside of her small chest, cavernous blackness washing over her, blacker than the snake-caves at home, where hundreds of hooded vipers roiled in pits, so lethargic from lovemaking the villagers were able to gather dozens, severing heads for the shaman's soothsaying stew, keeping the torsos to be stuffed with roots and spices, even those caves, entered with the village flashlight and flaming torches, were sunny airy places next to this void, as she backed away from the jeep, tripping over a rock, trying to reveal nothing to the sisters watching from the shack, blinded by tears she squeezed back into her eyeballs: she could not abandon her family or the mamasan in whose callused hands their fate and her shredded dignity was palmed.

"You go ...?" he said helplessly, sitting against the hot-backed seat, watching her head inside the dim shack, no backward look, no goodbye or thank you, and he felt the square weight of money in his pocket, folded and meant for her family; then she came back out and her voice caught and he did not make her say it, digging out the damp wad and giving it to her, trying to brush his fingertips against her palm, failing, and then she was gone again, still silent, a blind sheet of white agony and mind-crushing jealousy coursing over his eyes like a dropping curtain in an old-time movie theater, and he could only think that the mamasan be damned, he would be back that night.

But he did not go back that night. From the promenade, he couldn't see any twinkling Christmas lights, and wondered, had it all been the demonic dream of an evil god – had she meant nothing she said, been no more than professional in all she'd done, and would she eye him blankly if he entered the karaoke shack again, should he drive away forever right now, had his mind come unhinged at last, but, oh, he had to know, and even if it was only illusion, it didn't matter and he didn't care, because an existence without her was the illusion, and if it was all make-believe, he'd give up all pretense to reality, glug down bottles until he ended himself, but: even in the face of the sweaty day of mind-pulverizing doubt, he could not bring himself to disbelieve the promises and the words of love she'd repeated and offered, and so he would believe her, picturing her face the last time he'd seen it, that spoke of a lifetime of pain endured; how unbearably difficult her life must've been – look what she had to do to survive – how strong his brave little girl was! If she could take it, so could he. He would wait. New wad of cash in his pocket, he drank until he was sick over the railing of the promenade, and lost his way home among the swooping and swaying street lights and the leper glare of starlight. He awoke to head-tearing brain ache and speculations about how often she'd been a rental last night and how worthless he was to let it happen; she must hate him, surely it had been a test, to see if he would really go away, and he'd failed thunderously, she'd never consent to see him again, and he knew he had to go, that night, before surrendering the last shards of sanity.

The mamasan told her she was no longer permitted to leave the karaoke shack, stupid as she was, and if this cost her and her family some money, it would remind her not to be so stupid again. Her night was mechanical, a trader and a ship hand, their hands rough as dried coconut shells on her skin still fresh with boxida-memory, a couple hours in the bamboo shacks, money collected and the mamasan silent, her sisters, old and young, also silent, not even asking how much she'd raked the boxida over the coals for, and he didn't come, and there were moments, watching the black river outside, that she feared he didn't care after all, his sugar-laced words falsehoods, like the agent's, promising her a job as a maid in the big house of a rich man where she'd be well-taken care of; but she could not make herself believe her boxida had lied, and as the shack closed down, the first sister broke the silence, ordering her to carry the sewer buckets they'd saved up for her down to the river, the other sisters laughing and yammering, and she knew being with her boxida had sent her straight to the bottom, where she'd stay, probably even beyond next week when the new girl got here, and her future: the bamboo shacks until she was used up, then back to the toil and child-bearing of the village, and, oh, how staggering a chance was gone; she sloshed the sludgy sewage into the river to a great cloud of black flies, which squabbled on her bare shoulders and thighs and perched on her eyelashes, and on the last of a dozen trips, the second sister tripped her, warm gooey sewage from splattering all over her.

"Well how about that," said the first sister. "Shit still sticks to a boxida-fucker."

More peals of laughter from her sisters; she washed herself with scoopfuls of tepid water in the toilet, and the bouncer, gaze gone from protective to predatory, was waiting for her when she finished, throwing her face-down on his sleeping pallet alongside the karaoke shack, and forcing himself inside her before she could gasp, ramming her head into the tin wall, and when he finished, he wiped himself off on her shirt before grunting and throwing her out, and limping to her sleeping quarters she would have burned down her village to have back the moment when she could have gotten in the jeep with her boxida, and gone forever far away.

—3—

The next night he came. A uniformed gaggle of beer-swilling Thai cops were wailing songs and feeling up all the sisters but her – she'd not been allowed to approach the lucrative group, a coincidence for which she now praised the lucky spirits; the mamasan, fearing to stir the waters in the cops' unpredictable presence, barked at her to get beer down his throat and keep it short back in the bamboo shacks, the bouncer watching on attentive toes in the doorway.

He grabbed for her hand and said, "You come with me. Away from here. We go."

She said, "Mamasan say cannot."

"I say can. I take you. I take you now."

She put a hand on his arm and said, "First come with me."

She led him past the cops, who hooted and shouted "Hello!" to him, thinking it great fun that foreigners, too, should enjoy the national pastime, past baleful mamasan stirring cricket stew at the fire, to a bamboo shack.

She said, "If go with you, must never come back."

"Yes. Never come back to this place. I take you away. I take care."

"But where we go?"

"To far far away. To where you know."

"But, I not know here. They follow, they find." She thought about it. It didn't take long. She'd been thinking all day. "We go that way" – she pointed north – "in your car. To a town I hear of, called Lasan Sep. Can take boat over river. Into my country. I cannot stay here, but we go my country, can stay. Stay with you."

"Lasan Sep," he repeated. "I understand. We go."

"Wait. Have many people now. Mamasan, she see, she very angry. Maybe police follow us. We wait. They go soon. Wait."

She slipped out of the shack, and he waited, thinking she was going to gather her things, listening to the cops cackle and the girls squeal. Then she was back, with a bundle wrapped in a checkered rag, which she undid in the half light, which was a pistol. The bouncer's, kept between his sleeping pallet and the tin wall which she'd seen last night. Squat, black, greasy, loaded.

"I have this, she not stop us," she said, cheeks shining, looking at him beside her on the platform.

"Passport for us," he said.

Heart pounding against the back of his teeth, he hefted it, weight familiar – he'd taken a course with his ex-wife after a rash of break-ins in their neighborhood – giving it back to her, he could see their passport was familiar to her, too. He thought about removing the clip, decided not to. They lay down on the platform, faces so close their noses almost touched and their visages blurry in each other's eyes, oily gun on the rag between them, arms draped across each other, waiting for the cops to take the girls to a hotel they held a controlling interest in down the way, listening for the mamasan, who didn't come, being too busy attending to the cops' currency, the bouncer out on the cot idly watching the night river. In the bamboo shack neither spoke, waiting, until finally plastic chairs scraped over concrete, boots clacked and giggles turned to murmurs and in various vehicles emblazoned with official insignia, the cops left with the younger sisters, leaving the two older sisters, of whose charms they'd already grown tired.

"We go," she said, and did not turn away when he slobbered

in her mouth, a practice she found repulsive but knew he took as a sign of love.

"We go," he said, and they went down to the karaoke shack, her with the pistol, insisting, since no one'd believe a boxida required a gun to take what he wanted, her thin arm quaking.

The mamasan was in the main room, watching the two disgruntled older sisters clear up the mess, reckoning their usefulness to be much exaggerated if they were passed over by marks as easy as drunk cops, and thinking the little girl better have a pile of money on her, long as she'd been back there with the boxida, whittling down the already paltry amount to be forwarded to the girl's family, and seeing them come in, had to brush at her eyes, not believing she the little girl could be an arm's reach away with a gun pointed at her heart.

"Step back, old hag," she said to the mamasan. "We're getting out of here and I'm never coming back and I don't want to hear a sound."

"You little bitch," said the mamasan. "After everything I did for you. You think I won't track you down to that miserable mud puddle you call home, that I won't cut out your filthy tongue and ..."

The gun went off, nearly bucking out of her hand, the two older sisters screaming like dumb animals being flayed, clanking heads at the sight of the black pool spreading out from the supine mamasan, too shocked to run, and then she advanced on them, and the gun went off twice, and the two older sisters joined the mamasan on the floor.

"Jesus Christ!" he yelled, wrenching the gun away, hearing only pounding ringing in his head, whirling to a blurry movement, the bouncer running inside brandishing a tire iron, like one of those targets at the pistol range, cardboard cutout on a wire whizzing at you, and he fired twice, the bouncer's momentum toppling him over a table to fall on the mamasan; and then into the doorway tripped another figure, a cop, who'd been taking a squat in the bushes, unsteady on unsober legs; his first shot went over the cop's head, but the second and third did not, and then, in the receding reverberating din, the only sound was the clomping buffalo, loose from its tether and loping away.

A twitching older sister, choking on her own blood, knocked a glass off the table, which shattered into pieces that glinted in the black pools, and he watched her go into the cooking area where she smashed open the lacquered box beneath the Buddha-image, grabbing a neatly rubber-banded handful of cash and handing it to him, and then they were out of the karaoke shack, his brain yet to establish the veracity of his vision, into the jeep and down the dusty road, Christmas lights blinking in the rearview for a long-lasting second, to the familiar left and right turns, swerving past the cops at the checkpoint standing under a streetlight's pool of pus in the road, wondering at what they'd heard, back through the town where he did not brake for a crippled old dog too slow to get out of the way, into the dark night, moon invisible, headed north for Lasan Sep.

—4—

It was dark when they got to Lasan Sep the next day, past traffic cops who did not hear their hard-pounding hearts, abandoning the jeep down a dark side street, the entirety of their possessions on their bodies; they bought half a dozen bottles of water and drank them in another dark alley. The town was set high above the river, dyke running down to the riverbank, with stairs down to the narrow longtail boats, most flying Lao flags, weighed down to the water line with teak logs, lights of the Lao town on the opposite bank barely visible in the glare of Lasan Sep's night market, which extended from the dyke walkway to the temple gates, overflowing the streets and side streets of the town center with bulging stalls, stocked with goods of plastic practicality for the locals and cultural cut-outs for the tourists, the first he'd seen since Bangkok, wandering the narrow walkways with floppy hats and chubby legs and clutching backpacks and fanny packs and each other; he pulled her behind a stall proffering transistor radios, mangoes, and boiled duck's blood, slit-eyed stall owner obese in an orange sarong shrieking out sales pitches, and he told her to meet him at the temple gates, after she'd arranged things – he wanted to set a time, but when he unstrapped his watch, she stared at him confusedly, so he just shoved some bills in her hands, and she took them and disappeared into the teeming market, transfigured into a local shopper lookalike; he found an international ATM and drew out all it'd give, then wandered the market aimlessly, feeling as though a target was painted on his head, buying a small Buddha-image, stall owner saying it "give to you the good luck", hoping there was enough for the both of them, pretending to paw through souvenir stands and buying a couple T-shirts that seemed to be tiny enough for her, before a paroxysm of panic shivered through him that this singled him out.

A badly washed-out fax of his passport photo (there was no photo of her, only a sketchy written description) hung in the police box at the edge of the market with an official bulletin that advised the pair were thought to be headed west, based on the trembling suggestion of the youngest sister, who'd been waiting for the squatting cop and dived on a mash of still-warm buffalo dung when the shots went off; she'd watched the pair drive off, babbling all to the cops who clapped cuffs on her, a material witness with reason to flee, not to mention being an illegal alien and a possible scapegoat, but the cops in Lasan Sep were at the moment otherwise occupied, circulating through the market collecting their weekly protection fee and customary drink.

She went down to the river, skimpy outfit drawing looks, where she spoke to a group of boatmen squatting on the riverbank, waiting for their loads to be winched up the dyke, smoking hand-rolled Lao tobacco and muttering about the day's currents and ever-rising price of diesel. They balked when she mentioned the boxida and wanting to wait until the market lights were out and she watched helplessly as the news spread, the most exciting chatter on the riverbank since the river ferry, overloaded with migrant workers headed for the sugarcane and tamarind harvests, had capsized; she could only wait, squatting alone on the riverbank, turned away from the dyke and meeting no one's eyes, until a few bobbing chins led her to a boatman who muttered a price of two thousand baht, a ludicrous amount, but he'd said not to quibble, so she peeled off half, and told the boatman he'd get the rest on the other side. The boatman demanded another five hundred, which she handed over, trying not to think of how many eyes were following this transaction, and then she went back up the stairs, same pack of eyes following her from the riverbank, the chatter making it up and over the dyke minutes after she did.

She found him feigning an examination of carved wooden frog at a stand near the gates, fingers unsteady with steady-gnawing worry and guts wrung out with missing her; when she came he dropped the frog, hugging her tight to him, she watching wildly over his shoulder, caressing the back of his neck, whispering that he must stop this at once, then the two walked swiftly away, to the great annoyance of the stall owner, whose goods he'd disturbed in their entirety during the half hour he'd been there; they bought curries and rice in plastic to-go sacks, she pointing and trying to speak as little as possible to cloak her poor vernacular, and then they walked away from market, neither understanding the chatter that swirled through the market triangulating their position, around a bend to sit on a pile of logs outside a lumber warehouse, dipping rice into steaming bags of curry, leaning against each other and looking out over the inky Mekong cutting a wide swath of oily dark between feeble Lao lights and bright Thai ones and then, unable to stop with the touching, they made feverish love in impossible positions on the stack, ignoring the mosquitoes and rough-cutting teak, after which she sat on his lap, him feeling none of her slight weight, until the market lights began snapping off and the Mekong seemed to rise out of the dim gloom, implacable and ready to swallow their world, and they went back around the bend and headed down the stairs, where she recognized a figure squatted by an empty boat.

"That is him," she said.

They got into the boat, pupils wide in the dark, the boatman firing up the engine and as they turned into the current, stark spotlights beamed down from the dyke and flashlights came bumpily down the stairs, megaphone-garbled voice bellowing words neither understood, but both comprehended perfectly well. She hissed at the boatman and they clutched each other as plinging bullets spattered around them; the cops, bad shots at the best of times, were reeling from the drinks proffered by the stall owners, but they used up all the ammunition they had. The engine sputtered and died and the prow turned down with the current and the boatman was slumped over, hand trailing in the water, black stain spreading over the bench.

The town disappeared behind the bending river, no sounds of pursuit, the police patrol boat half a dozen kilometers upriver, its sole operator at a karaoke shack eyeing the merchandise and swigging beer and as the boat spun in the swift eddies, he took the boatman's hand out of the water and nearly capsized the thing trying to shift the corpse overboard; she crawled over the corpse and squatted next to the warm engine but did not know how to start it nor in the dark was there any way to learn, so she crawled back to him, not looking at the inky water with its unknown evils, and they watched for where the current would take them, paddling hard when it looked like it might be to the Thai side, though they only succeeded in spinning the boat in semicircles. Then the river veered to the right, and they heard rushing torrents, and then came giant jagged silhouettes overhanging the river, rock outcroppings the boat slid under, hull scraping horribly as the water shallower out, and they flattened themselves down, he on top of her, boat rattling and wobbling against the rocks, before popping back out into the current, tilting madly, long tailed propeller catching on something, boat jolting to a halt, marooned and shivering, and they could hear rapids rumbling ahead, which he could not imagine the shallow wooden craft could survive, and she held back whimpers, knowing will was futile in the face of spirits you were powerless against, the warm skin of her boxida on hers and home so close, and her toes were wet – the boat had sprung a leak.

He held her and tried to gauge how far away Laos was; he doubted she could swim, but they could not chance the rapids, so as the water in the boat reached his ankles, he said,

"We go. Swim."

"Oh," she said.

"You must. You stay with me."

"I stay with you," she said.

He edged himself over the edge of the boat while she gripped his arms, warm breath on his face, to bash his knees on rocky riverbed, a foot below the hull; he felt around, riverbed solid and tepid water shallow, and he stood slowly as she watched, at first thinking he was now revealing secret powers, then she saw, and whooping leaned over to the boatman and extracted the bills from a pocket, hand getting sticky, and clambered over to her boxida, sharp-pointed rocks stabbing through the thin soles of her sandals as they picked their way ashore and up an outcropping to a trail leading into the forest beyond, where the night sounds were as she knew them.

ACKNOWLEDGEMENTS

Thanks go out first to my wife, Nok, for enduring my early morning and late night shiftings with grace, and for always being sure this day would come. None of the stories here would have been possible without my first and best readers, Timothy McCrystle in Thailand and Brad Green in America. I'd also like to thank fellow writers Les Edgerton, Sean O'Kane, Roxane Gay, Ron Brown, Norman Savage, David Rothman, Douglas Glover, David James Keaton, Chris Rhatigan, Joe Clifford, Steve Weddle, Todd Robinson and Donigan Merritt, for helping me fight the good fight. I'd also like to acknowledge my children, Ada and Waylon, who kept me real in the real world.

My gratitude is also due to Ce Merrigan, my mom, for all the love and encouragment over the years. Somsak Tangreungsri, Rattinan Boonyasitwikul, Pa Bin and Phor El Ngoenhom, Lung Taem, Toby MacGuire, and Brent Rossow in Thailand. Hiroshi Gake, Ishimoto-san, Machiko Yokoyama, Tomomi Moriwaki, Minori Sawada, Kenji Konno, Sam Goodman, Rio Hernandez, Ted Hunter and Richard Robson in Japan. My colleagues and professors at Eastern Wyoming College and the University of Wyoming, and family and friends throughout Wyobraska and beyond.

Thanks also Brian Lindenmuth, for taking on and editing this meandering collection, and Eric Beetner and Ron Earl Phillips for all the drafted and re-drafted covers and interiors. I'd also like acknowledge all those editors and readers who saw fit to publish my stuff, in print and online.

ABOUT THE AUTHOR

Court Merrigan's short stories are out or coming soon in *Thuglit*, *Needle*, *Weird Tales*, *Plots With Guns*, *Big Pulp*, *Noir Nation*, and a bunch of others. His story "The Cloud Factory," which appeared in *PANK*, was nominated for a Spinetingler Award. He also runs the Bareknuckles Pulp Department at Out of the Gutter. After a decade of the nomadic life in East Asia he lives in Wyoming with his family.